A PROMISE FOR TOMORROW

When Hope has to close her beloved shop, she reluctantly accepts her godmother's suggestion and returns to her family's roots in southern Scotland. Although caring for Mr Jackson is challenging, surprisingly, it's fun to do, and gradually she is able to put her business disaster into perspective. She is drawn into village life, and wonders if she could grow particularly close to farmer's son Robbie. But first she must sort out some long-hidden family secrets . . .

GILLIAN VILLIERS

A PROMISE
FOR TOMORROW

Complete and Unabridged

LINFORD
Leicester

First published in Great Britain in 2010

First Linford Edition
published 2011

British Library CIP Data

Villiers, Gillian.
   A promise for tomorrow. - -
(Linford romance library)
1. Villages- -Scotland- -Fiction.
2. Farmers- -Scotland- -Fiction.
3. Family secrets- -Fiction.
4. Love stories. 5. Large type books.
I. Title II. Series
823.9′2–dc22

ISBN 978–1–4448–0771–4

Published by
F. A. Thorpe (Publishing)
Anstey, Leicestershire

Set by Words & Graphics Ltd.
Anstey, Leicestershire
Printed and bound in Great Britain by
T. J. International Ltd., Padstow, Cornwall

This book is printed on acid-free paper

An Opportunity Arises For Hope

'I've got just the job for you,' Aunt Susie said. Susie Ashbury was Hope's godmother, not an aunt, but after so many years Hope found it hard to get out of the habit of calling her that.

'But I'm not looking for a job,' said Hope, bemused.

'It's just what you need. You can't do anything about the shop at the moment and you need to get away from Brighton. A complete change of scenery will do you the world of good.'

Hope remembered her mother used to say how bossy Susie was. This was the first time she had experienced it herself.

'But . . . I need to be here. To sort things out with the accountant and the solicitor and . . . and everyone.' Hope shuddered. The legal wrangling was just one of the awful things about having a business that went wrong. Her lovely, exciting, vibrant shop, that Aladdin's cave of cottons and silks and lace, was no more.

'I'm sure you don't need to be on hand for that. You'll be amazed to find how much can be sorted out by phone, or even by e-mail. Far better to get away and keep yourself busy with something completely different.'

Hope allowed herself the glimmer of optimism. It would be lovely to escape, even if only for a while. When she had heard Aunt Susie's voice on the phone, she had expected an invite to stay for a week or two. A job was completely unexpected.

'What kind of job?' she said. She couldn't help herself.

'Do you remember old Mr Jackson at Kirkside House? The large red sand-stone house down by the church?'

'Not really.' Hope realised it was years since she had visited her godmother.

Whilst her mother had been alive Susie had always come to them, and somehow after her death this pattern had continued. Susie enjoyed the contrast the south coast of England gave to her life in a quiet Scottish village. She had, of course, invited Hope to visit, but the timing had never seemed quite right.

'It's a wonderful old house. A bit run down now, of course, the poor dear can't take care of it the way he used to and he doesn't like to admit he needs help. Which he needs more than ever just now. He had a nasty fall last week and smashed his hip. It was a good thing actually, although you don't like to say that, do you? He'd been refusing to go in for the op for years, but this time they had to do it. He's still in hospital at the moment, but they say he'll need to go to a nursing home for convalescence. He's refusing point blank. He's determined to go back to his own home.' Even when Susie had something important to say, it took her a while to get to the point. She was so interested in the details of other people's lives.

Hope found herself smiling as she listened. It was a while since she had smiled and it felt good.

Susie continued, 'A few of the neighbours would be happy to rally around and lend a hand, but to begin with he's going to need a bit more looking after than we can manage. He really needs someone around twenty-four hours a day, and that's where you come in.'

'Me?' Hope was genuinely alarmed. She had been wondering if Susie was setting her up for a little house-sitting.

She could cope with that. But looking after an elderly man? Nursing? She didn't think so.

'Yes. You wouldn't need to nurse him or anything,' said Susie, as though reading her mind. 'The district nurses will come in regularly to check on him, change his dressings and so on. You would just need to look after him.'

'But Susie, I don't know anything

about doing that. You and Mum trained as nurses, not me.'

'I know, but you've got the right attitude, and that's what counts. You'll be a carer, not a nurse, and you've always been a very caring girl, Hope. A good girl.'

Hope wasn't sure about that, but decided not to argue right now.

'I don't know . . . ' Getting away from the mess of her life in Brighton was attractive, but did she really want to go so far away, live in a large house, with an elderly invalid? 'What would I have to do?'

'Not a lot,' said Susie breezily. 'Cook his meals, keep him company. In return he would provide you with accommodation and a small salary. Didn't you say you were having to give up your flat?'

'Yes,' said Hope looking about sadly. The flat was tiny, but it was hers. She had had such great plans for it. 'It's on the same lease as the shop. I need to be out by the end of the month.'

'This is ideal, then. Mr Jackson won't be discharged for another five to seven days, ample time for you to get yourself up here. You do what you need to do, then let us know when to expect you. Simon and I are so looking forward to seeing more of you.'

'I'll need to think about it,' said Hope, but somehow she knew the decision had already been made.

★ ★ ★

As Hope turned off the busy motorway onto the winding roads approaching St. Ann's Bridge, she felt a quiver of excitement in the pit of her stomach. Such green hills, so many trees, so few houses. This place was very different to the bustling streets of Brighton. It was like entering another world, a beautiful peaceful one. She wondered why it had taken her so long to come back.

She drove slowly, partly because the roads were narrow and partly because she wasn't entirely sure of her way. But partly, too, for the sheer pleasure of being here.

To her surprise and relief she found Aunt Susie's house without too much difficulty. It was a large 1930s bungalow near the centre of the village. When Susie's husband, Simon, had been the local doctor, the surgery had been attached to the house. She remembered Susie saying a new health centre had been built not long before Simon retired and his old surgery had been made into a guest wing.

'Plenty of room for you to stay,' she had said, during one of her many attempts to entice Hope north. 'The children come and visit and say it's very comfortable, but they're not here as often as we'd like. Not that I'm complaining.' And Susie had launched happily into accounts of the life of her three offspring. Hope had heard so much about them she felt she knew them well, despite not having seen them for ten years or more.

She parked the car carefully in the

driveway. Before she had opened her door, Susie was hurrying towards her, arms outstretched.

'Hope, darling, it's lovely to see you.' She gave her a hug, engulfing her in the familiar perfume. She was tiny, at least a head shorter than Hope, but she seemed to encircle the younger woman. Hope felt safe.

Uncle Simon arrived more slowly. He had put on weight and lost more hair since Hope had seen him last, at her mother's funeral, but he was still the same solid dependable Uncle Simon. He shook her hand and offered to help her with her cases.

'Don't worry about those now,' said Susie, tucking her arm through Hope's and leading her up the steps to the front door. 'I'm sure Hope wants to freshen herself up and then have a nice cup of tea. And I want to hear all her news.'

'Do remember not everyone has your stamina,' said her husband wryly. 'Hope has had a long drive. Perhaps she'd like a rest before the inquisition?'

'Of course she won't. A young thing like her? Why, in the old days I'd drive all the way south on my own and after a quick meal we'd be straight out to the theatre. Do you remember, dear? Your mother knew I missed things like that living out in the sticks here. We had such fun on my visits, didn't we?'

'We did,' agreed Hope, feeling a lump in her throat. It was easy to forget those happy times when things had been so difficult for her mother towards the end. And Hope hadn't been there for her as she should have been.

She allowed Susie to usher her inside and turned her thoughts determinedly towards this new life ahead.

★   ★   ★

'How do you think she is?' Susie asked her husband that evening as they settled down with their usual nightcaps. Simon had a very small whisky and Susie had one of her lovely herbal teas. She had tried to persuade him to try them, so far without success.

'She's looking very well,' said Simon cautiously. Of course, as a retired GP, it was Hope's health he thought of first. 'Tired, naturally. I'm glad she's taken herself off to bed early. Just what she needed.'

'Yes, she's better than I feared,' agreed Susie. 'She sounded so low when I spoke to her. Not surprising, with her so-called friend letting her down like that. I got the impression Hope put her heart and soul into the shop.'

'Not to mention a fair amount of money,' said Simon. 'I wish we had been more involved in the setting up of the business. A partnership can be very risky, especially when one partner proves to be so unreliable.'

'That's behind her now,' said Susie firmly. 'We can't change the past but we can help her pick up the pieces and look to the future. This little job with Mr Jackson is a very useful first step.

I've got definite plans for Hope.'

'Now, now, you promised you wouldn't meddle.' Simon frowned across at his wife.

She smiled brightly back. 'I don't meddle, dear. I just like to give a helping hand. After all, she is my goddaughter. Now our three are settled and off our hands I can give her my full attention.'

Simon groaned.

'The first thing is to get her to know her roots,' continued Susie, ignoring him. 'I always told her mother I didn't agree with keeping her away from Scotland. Elspeth did a good job of bringing her up more or less on her own, but a person likes to know where they come from. It grounds them. Yes, definitely, I think we should start with Hope's family.'

'I thought the whole point was, she doesn't have any family,' said Simon, looking confused.

'No relatives left alive,' agreed his wife, wondering for the umpteenth time why men were so obtuse. 'But she's got an awful lot of dead ones buried down in the kirkyard. She knows lots about her father's family, but as far as I can tell, she doesn't know anything about these ones.'

Susie thought of the tall, slight girl she had eventually enticed back to St. Ann's Bridge. She was a pretty thing, with her delicate features and long brown hair. She looked nothing like her mother at the same age, in either appearance or style. Poor Elspeth had always had such a buttoned-up appearance, neat and tidy skirts and blouses, never seen in slacks. Hope, too, seemed to prefer skirts, but hers were long, floaty affairs, no doubt made by the girl herself, from brightly-coloured soft material. Susie thought her own daughter, Sarah, would call it 'the layered look'. It suited Hope, but would probably look a little unusual up here.

Susie smiled. That was a good thing. She wanted people to notice her guest.

'Tomorrow I'll take her to the

hospital to meet Mr Jackson,' she said.

'Now that is a good idea,' said Simon. 'Much better than graveyards.'

Susie ignored the criticism. 'I wonder how she feels about dogs. I forgot to ask her. Mr Jackson will want Lucy back as soon as he gets home.'

'Who's looking after her?'

'The Mackenzies. They are a nice family. They offered to have Lucy straight away and with their farm being next door to Kirkside it was the least disruption for the poor old thing. Did I not tell you that young Robbie Mackenzie got special permission from the hospital to take Lucy in for a visit? Now wasn't that kind of him?'

'Goodness, how times change. Imagine allowing a dog in a hospital!'

'Hospitals are much more accommodating than in our day.' Susie was delighted about that. The visit from Mr Jackson's bearded collie had done him more good than anything else she could think of.

She nodded to herself and took a last

sip of the lemon and ginger. 'Yes, I think things are going rather well. And you know what, it wouldn't be a bad thing if I introduced Hope to that nice Robbie Mackenzie tomorrow as well.'

'Susie,' said her husband. 'No meddling, remember?'

She patted his hand. 'As if I would.' There was no point in trying to explain. Simon had never been able to understand the difference between meddling and giving people a nudge in the right direction.

Robbie Feels Family Pressure

'Families! Who needs them?' thought Robbie Mackenzie as he headed out for his early morning jog. He certainly didn't. All they did was nag, nag, nag.

OK, so he could see that Lucy, their foster dog, needed a walk, but he could do that when he got back. His mum knew he went too far and too fast when he ran. She thought he was crazy to do it, but it was his choice, wasn't it? He could easily take old Lucy out for a stroll later, although his mother would more than likely have done so already. And probably enjoyed herself in the process. But she just couldn't resist trying to organise everyone in sight.

His mother was bad, but his father was worse. Far worse.

He'd started again last night with, 'I

thought now you were back home we'd see more of you around the place. I don't know why you needed to go and find yourself a job miles away, there's plenty to do here.'

That was the problem. There wasn't plenty to do on the Holm Farm. Yes, at certain times of year they were frantically busy, but the reality of the farm was it hardly made enough money to support two men, let alone three. And with Luke about to get married he would need to take a reasonable salary from the place. His father must realise there would be nothing left for Robbie, even if he had wanted to work there.

'I trained in countryside management because that is what I want to do,' he had replied, trying to keep his tone mild. It was a real bonus that a job had come up so close to home. He had thought his parents would be pleased, for goodness sake. They'd moaned enough when he was based in the far north.

'It was always your grandfather's

dream that you boys would take over the farm between you. That's why he struggled to take on the extra land, build it up to what it is today, one of the biggest holdings in the area.'

'It's great what Grandad did,' Robbie had said through gritted teeth. 'But there still isn't enough work for more than two people. First Grandad and you, now you and Luke.'

'There is always more work to do on a farm,' said his father gloomily. His wind-reddened face looked tired and Robbie realised how the ginger hair was already turning to white.

'I'm happy to help out when I can, but you have to admit it, Dad, there isn't enough money to give me a proper income, no matter how much work I do.'

'That's the point, isn't it? Money is the only thing that matters to young people these days. Whatever happened to working for the joy of it? You young people want to clock off at five and go gallivanting to the pub, or playing that fancy music you're so interested in. I don't call that work.'

Robbie had managed to extricate himself after that, but the conversation had depressed him. Nothing he did was ever right as far as his father was concerned. The man must have been born critical. He didn't know how his brother could put up with working with him day in and day out.

He sighed and decided to concentrate on the track ahead of him and not the family he had left behind.

When he returned an hour later he was in much better spirits, which just went to prove he had been right to go out.

'Any breakfast going begging?' he asked as he entered the kitchen. He could smell bacon so he knew there was.

'It's in the warming oven,' said his mother, trying but failing to look annoyed. 'Your father and brother ate half-an-hour ago and they're back out to the dairy. You know I haven't got all day to wait around and cook for you.'

'Of course you haven't,' agreed Robbie, wiping his face with a towel. 'But you know you love to do it.'

'Hmm.'

Robbie retrieved a plate from the bottom of the Rayburn and inhaled appreciatively. It was laden with eggs and bacon, cooked tomato and beans. 'This looks brilliant. You deserve a hug.'

His mother waved him away. 'Wait until you've cleaned yourself up.'

'Where's Lucy?'

'Asleep on the rug in the sitting room. I took her around the near field and that was about all she could manage, poor old thing.'

'We should get a dog of our own, then you could take it for proper walks.'

'I don't have the time,' said his mother, pretending to be grumpy. 'At least Lucy only needs short walks. Which reminds me, I've a hundred and one things to do in the office and I still haven't seen to the hens, I'd better get on. And shouldn't you be heading off to work?'

'I start at ten today,' said Robbie, digging in happily to his food.

'It's no wonder your father doesn't consider it a real job . . . ' muttered his mother as she headed out.

Robbie sighed. His father didn't consider anything other than farming a real job. But Robbie loved his work as a countryside ranger. For most of the time he was entirely on his own, and if he was rostered to do educational sessions in schools, or take groups out for walks, then he was the boss. It was ideal.

What he loved best of all was playing the fiddle, but, despite what his father thought, he was sensible enough to realise he couldn't make a living from that. He did, however, have one or two ideas about doing a bit more with his music. He hadn't played seriously since he left college. Now he was back home, it was time to start practising again and take it from there.

★   ★   ★

Hope was nervous about meeting Mr
Jackson. What if he didn't like her? She
would have come all this way for
nothing. It didn't matter that Susie
insisted he would love her, she couldn't
help worrying. She really wasn't used to
being around older people. Her poor
darling mother had only been in her
fifties when she died and there were no
grandparents on either side. As she
followed Susie, reluctantly, along the
disinfectant-scented hospital corridors,
she grew more and more doubtful.

Mr Jackson was a gaunt man in his
early eighties. He was propped up
uncomfortably in the high hospital bed
with some kind of cushion around his
injured hip.

When Hope was introduced he shook
her hand firmly and looked her up and
down. Her heart sank further. She
should probably have put on some
sensible, dull clothes. The maroon
velvet jacket with its sequins and

mirrors would have been unusual in Brighton, and certainly turned a few heads here.

'Pleased to meet you,' she whispered.

'Hmm? What was that?' The elderly man frowned.

'I said I'm very pleased to meet you.'

'Good, good. I'm pleased to meet you, too, if it means they'll let me out of this place. You go and find out what they're saying about that now, Susie, I can't make out half of what's going on. They never give you a straight answer and they're all too young.'

'There's nothing wrong with young doctors,' said Susie. 'Simon says he doesn't know where we would be without them. And perhaps you would get on better if you wore your hearing aid.'

'More trouble than it's worth,' said Mr. Jackson briskly. 'Now, off you go and I can talk to the lassie here.'

To Hope's dismay, Susie did as she was told.

'So you're Elspeth Calvert's girl,' said the man. He examined her closely. He might be hard of hearing, but there didn't seem to be anything wrong with his sight.

'Yes, that's right.'

'Sit down, sit down. I don't bite you know. You may as well look as though you mean to stay.'

Hope perched on the edge of a hard plastic chair. 'How are you feeling?' she said, remembering to raise her voice.

'No' so grand. But we don't want to talk about that. Both your parents are dead, aren't they? I'm sure that's what Susie Ashbury said.'

'Yes. My father died when I was eleven and my mother when I was at college.' Hope had given this explanation so often now it almost didn't hurt. The shock of her father's sudden death, from which her mother had never quite recovered, had cast a shadow over her teens. Even worse had been her mother's own serious illness which she had kept from Hope for far too long.

'So you're an orphan. Cannae be easy.'

'Susie is my godmother. She's been

23

very good to me. And I have friends.'
Hope tried not to think of how her
supposed best friend, Amy, had let her
down.

'Family's aye important,' said Mr
Jackson in his brusque way. 'I've none
left close by so I ken that fine. My boy
emigrated to Australia. Fine for holi-
days when I was able to get out and
about, but now it's just too far. Hardly
know my grandchildren.'

'That's a shame.'

Mr Jackson nodded. His cheeks were
drawn and his neck so thin that Hope
was surprised it could support the
weight of his high-domed head. She
realised how frail he was, for all his
brusqueness, and some of her nervous-
ness disappeared.

'Now, have you met my Lucy?'

Hope was momentarily confused. Was
this some relative Susie had forgotten to
mention? And then she remembered.
Lucy was the dog.

'No, not yet. The people who are
looking after her are bringing her round

this evening. I'm looking forward to it.' That was true. Hope had never had a dog. Her mother thought it would be too much trouble, but she had often longed for one.

'Sooner I get home the better. She won't like being away from her own routine. You go and make friends with her and settle yourself in the house. I'm getting out of this place by the end of the week, one way or another. Ah, here's Susie, she'll know what's going on.'

'They say they need to wait for the Consultant to see you,' said Susie, pulling up a slightly more comfortable chair beside Hope. 'But from what I can gather from Sister they don't see any reason why he should want you to stay much longer. She talked about organising a 'package of care' for you, but when I explained about Hope she said that should make things a lot quicker.'

'Good. I want to be out of here by Friday. Can you have the lass settled in by then?'

'Of course,' said Susie approvingly.

'We'll have everything ready for you. I can see that you and my goddaughter are going to get along famously.'

'She'll do,' said Mr Jackson and laid his head back on the pillow, apparently dismissing them.

Hope was relieved to be out of the hospital. Illness made her tense. In her experience, when people went in to hospital they didn't get better. But Mr. Jackson was going to. He was going to be fine.

'He likes you,' said Susie happily.

Hope grinned. 'I think he'd accept anyone, as long as it meant he could get out of hospital.'

'Actually, I didn't want to mention this before, but he can be a bit awkward. If he hadn't liked you he would have said so. I'm very pleased with how that went.'

Hope wondered what on earth she had let herself in for, if this abrupt conversation was considered a resounding success. It was too late to back out now.

Getting In Touch With The Past

Hope followed Susie up the hill from the row of 'new' bungalows where she and Simon lived, to the older part of the village. She hardly knew this part at all, although she remembered once going to a service in a little old church at the end of a winding track. From what Susie had said, she presumed Mr Jackson's house would be near this. However, Susie led her past the turning clearly marked *Church and Graveyard*.

'I thought it would be down there,' she said, surprised.

'It is. In fact that's Kirkside you can see from the road. But I wanted to show you something else first.'

She continued on until they were past the end of the village then Susie pointed down a tiny track to the left.

'I don't suppose you've ever been down there, have you?' Her godmother looked at her consideringly.

'No,' said Hope, puzzled now. She pushed her long hair back over her shoulder and squinted through the gloom of the trees that overhung the track on both sides. 'Where does it lead?'

'That's Cleughbrae. Where your mother lived.'

Hope peered down the gloomy track, wondering why she was so surprised. She had known her mother had lived in St. Ann's Bridge since her adoption when she was three years old. Her adoptive parents had, however, died by the time Hope came along. Her mother had never spoken of her childhood or the house where she had grown up. When Hope had asked questions, her mother had said, 'you wouldn't be interested in that.' It was odd that Susie had brought her here now. She clearly thought Hope would be interested.

'What a funny little road,' said Hope doubtfully. The track was dark, scattered with loose stones and dead leaves. 'It looks as though it could lead to Hansel and Gretel's cottage.'

'The house isn't quite that picturesque,' said Susie with a snort of laughter. She turned back, no longer keen to continue with the tour. 'I'll take you to have a look when we have more time. Now, we'd better make a quick visit to Kirkside then I need to go home to make Simon's dinner.'

Kirkside proved to be more or less what Hope had expected. A large red-sandstone house standing foursquare in a generous garden, with an air of neglect that surely dated from before Mr Jackson's recent stay in hospital. The house smelt a little musty, but it wasn't unwelcoming.

'It's massive,' murmured Hope as her godmother took her rapidly through the four rooms and kitchen on the ground floor before leading her up the wide staircase.

'Yes. Lovely old place. Most of it is no longer used, as you can see.'

'My flat would have fitted into one of the smaller sitting rooms.'

'It'll be fun for you to live in a place with so much space.'

'As long as I don't get too used to it,' said Hope, as a warning to herself. She felt she was going to rather like this house.

Susie showed her the bedrooms, pointing out one looking down to the river which she had picked out for Hope's own use, and then went on to discuss how they could set up a bedroom on the ground floor for Mr Jackson until he could manage the stairs again. 'If he ever can. There are rather a lot of them, aren't there?' Susie frowned at the long sweep of steps, so different from the sensible layout of her own bungalow. 'I wonder if we could get a stair-lift installed?'

'And I wonder if Mr Jackson would ever agree to one.'

'How right you are!' Susie gave her a

hug. 'I'm so glad you understand him. He's a darling, but not the easiest of people. Right, best get off home. I wonder if we can persuade Robbie Mackenzie to help with the furniture removal? We'll ask him when he brings the dog around this evening. Now that's a very good idea.'

★ ★ ★

Robbie was a little late taking Lucy to the Ashburys'. He didn't see that it mattered, for goodness sake, he had said something along the lines of he would drop in around eight. But his mother was, unfortunately, a stickler for punctuality. When he was still eating his dinner at five-to-eight she had started to get agitated and when he hadn't left by five past she was all set to phone Susie Ashbury and tell her he would be late.

'It's only a five minutes walk,' he protested. 'And no one expects you to be absolutely on time.'

'I do,' said his mother firmly. 'I was brought up in a household where neither Mama nor Papa could ever be on time and I vowed not to be the same.'

'And I was brought up in a house where you and Dad are not only on time but usually early — and see what that has done for me. And come to think of it, Luke's not exactly punctual, is he?'

His mother cuffed him affectionately. 'Off you go. It'll take you more than five minutes, you know Lucy can't walk quickly these days.'

'Yes Mum, no Mum.' Robbie ducked sideways to avoid another cuff and, calling the grey-haired collie (twice, she was hard of hearing), he finally set off.

It was another lovely summer evening. The grass in the fields was long and waved gently in the slight breeze. If this dry spell continued they would be able to cut the hay soon. He looked forward to that. Harvest time was the one period when the farm could do with more than a couple of workers and, despite his father, he enjoyed helping out. Sometimes they worked on long into the twilight. There was always a thrill to getting in the hay, defeating the fickle Scottish weather.

Luke wanted to move over to doing more silage, as that wasn't so weather-dependent, but their father wouldn't hear of it. As far as he was concerned, silage was some new-fangled fad.

He rang the doorbell of the Ashburys' bungalow. After a moment Susie appeared and led him through the house and conservatory to a patio that looked over the sloping garden at the rear. It was all beautifully tended, unlike his parents' place. Being farmers, they never seemed to have time for neatness and flowers.

Sitting in the cane chairs were Dr Ashbury, looking a little greyer since Robbie had last seen him, and the girl who must be the house-cum-dog-sitter. Hope, that's what she was called. It had made him expect a small, plain, neat person which couldn't have been further from the truth.

The girl who rose to shake his hand was slight, but she was neither plain nor neat. She had dark eyes in a rather pale face and long wavy brown hair held back in a loose plait. She wore a sleeveless top of some kind of material that shimmered in the sunshine and a strange long skirt with an uneven hem. She wasn't classically pretty but she was arresting. And there was something else about her that made him want to look twice, a wistful sadness in her eyes.

He shook her slim hand and said, 'Pleased to meet you.' He meant it, too.

'Thank you. And you. And is this Lucy?' She spoke softly in an English accent he couldn't identify. He wished he had paid more attention when his mother was chattering about where the girl came from.

She had bent down, her long skirt swishing on the ground, and held out a hand to the bearded collie. 'Hello darling, are you Lucy? Are you going to say hello?'

'Yes, this is Lucy. Goodness knows how she can see anything with all that hair in her eyes but she seems to manage. She's a bit deaf though, you have to speak up.'

The collie had noticed Hope now and turned her large shaggy head to the proffered hand. She sniffed it, then licked it, then nudged with her head to be stroked.

'She likes you already,' said Susie Ashbury happily. 'I knew she would. Now, Robbie, have a seat. What can I get you to drink?'

Robbie hadn't intended to stay more than a few minutes, but he found he had changed his mind. He took a seat in one of the pretty chairs and accepted a shandy. He needed something thirst-quenching after the hard day's work on the hill.

Dr Ashbury chatted to him about how it felt returning to the area after living away, and the girl patted the dog and listened, asking an occasional question herself. He hoped this meant

35

she was interested and not just that she was being polite.

'How long have you been up here?' he asked, wanting to involve her more in the conversation.

'I only arrived yesterday.'

'Did you have a long way to come?'

'Quite a long way.' She smiled slightly. 'From Brighton, actually. It took me over nine hours but I did have a few stops.'

'Always sensible to take some breaks,' said Dr Ashbury. 'Every two to three hours would be my advice.'

'I've never been to Brighton,' he said, examining the girl. He wondered if everyone wore strange and colourful clothes down there. 'Is it nice?'

'It can be a fun place to live,' she said with a brief smile. Then she looked sad again. 'But I was glad to get away. Now I'm here I've realised perhaps I'm not really a city person. I loved the seafront in Brighton, it gives you a sense of space, but that's nothing to what you have around here.' She gestured to the valley that fell away below the garden and then to the rolling green hills beyond. 'This is beautiful. I don't know why my mother didn't want to come back more often.'

Robbie opened his mouth and then closed it again. He had just remembered something his mother had said about Elspeth McIlroy. If it was true, he wasn't surprised she hadn't liked to return to St. Ann's Bridge.

★　★　★

Hope was both worried and excited about moving into Kirkside. This would be the end of her short holiday with Susie and Simon and the beginning of her new 'job,' which was scary. On the other hand, it would be a step forward, a positive decision to move on after the fiasco of the shop. She needed to concentrate on that side of things and not worry whether she was really cut out to be a carer.

On the day of the move, Simon

accompanied them, to carry in Hope's suitcases (although she could have managed perfectly well herself) and to inspect their arrangements. Whilst he took the cases upstairs Hope and Susie ferried carrier bags of food into the kitchen.

The ringing of the front door bell heralded another arrival, which could only be Robbie Mackenzie, come to drop off Lucy and help rearrange the furniture.

Hope found herself unaccountably nervous at the thought of seeing him again. He had seemed such a self-possessed young man, charmingly at ease and good-looking in a Latin way that had seemed quite unexpected in the Scottish countryside. Susie had explained his mother was of Italian descent. This had made him seem all the more exotic.

Hope felt it was a terrible imposition asking him to help them move beds and wardrobes. You would never have dreamed of asking a neighbour to do something like that in Brighton or Bournemouth.

Now she followed Susie back into the wide entrance hall, rubbing her hands nervously on her patchwork skirt. Then she caught sight of Lucy, looking so forlorn with all that hair in her eyes, and she forgot to be concerned. She bent and put her hand out towards the old dog. 'How are you darling? How does it feel to be back in your home?'

Robbie watched this with a grin on his handsome face. Once again he wore jeans and a T shirt. He pushed the curly dark hair back from his face and said, 'Right, let's make a start, shall we? What was it you wanted me to move?'

He smiled at Hope who could feel herself begin to blush. Fortunately Susie took charge, as she was used to doing.

'We're converting the back sitting room into a bedroom for Mr Jackson. We don't want to risk him hurting himself on the stairs. Social services have provided a special bed for him, which is very good of them. That's already in there. We've managed to move out some of the furniture, but if you could shift the settee and that massive sideboard we'd appreciate it. And then we can go upstairs and see about moving some things down.'

The furniture was old and very solid. Hope wondered how on earth Robbie was going to manage to move it.

She needn't have worried. Robbie had no problem at all with items Hope and Susie could scarcely manage between them. For the heavier ones he needed Simon's help, but Hope suspected the younger man was doing most of the lifting.

Susie wanted to hang around and get in the way so Hope suggested they go and make a cup of tea. It was funny to see her decisive godmother dithering between her desire to oversee the two men and her obligation to help with the catering. Eventually duty won out and she followed Hope into the lovely square kitchen at the rear of the house.

'I do hope they're going to manage, I would never have let Simon come with us if I'd known he was going to get involved in lifting things. Now where did we put the tea bags?'

Hope began opening cupboards, trying to memorise where everything was kept. The kitchen was dominated by an old cream Aga, which had not yet been relit. Everything was functional, but well past its first flush of youth. Hope rather liked it, although Susie tutted over the lack of such essentials as a toaster and a microwave.

'At least there's an electric kettle,' said Hope. 'And look at these lovely cups and saucers. And what a wonderful old teapot!'

'That's a Wedgewood Blush Rose,' said Susie.

'Is it valuable?' asked Hope, putting it back down quickly.

'No more so than many of the other things here. Mr Jackson's wife, Millie, always said nice things were here to be used and I presume he's carried on the same way. Oh dear, what was that?' as a loud bang could be heard from the hallway. 'I do hope they're all right . . . '

'They're fine,' said Hope firmly, when the crash wasn't followed by shouting or yelling. Robbie Mackenzie was being remarkably restrained, she had noted, even when he trapped his thumb between a wardrobe and the wall.

Hope carried the refreshments into the front sitting room and Susie went to summon the men. This sitting room was lovely, south facing with a massive bay window flanked by rather faded, but still grand, green velvet curtains. There were a number of settees set around a generous coffee table. Glass display cabinets and fancy hard-backed chairs were set around the walls. Yes, thought Hope, looking about, she was going to enjoy staying here.

Robbie and Simon looked a little pink after their exertions, but soon recovered their breath and were happily helping themselves to gypsy creams and cups of tea. Lucy settled down at Robbie's feet. After a thorough examination of the house the collie had reluctantly accepted her master wasn't home.

'How's Luke getting on?' Susie asked Robbie. 'Wedding preparations going all right?'

Robbie let out a gusty sigh. 'I'm trying to keep out of it, so I'm probably not the right person to ask. All I can say is they seem to be taking up an awful lot of time.' He turned to Hope. 'Luke is my older brother. He and his fiancée, Claire, are getting married in September.' He sighed again. 'I'm his Best Man so Mum is forever on at me for my opinion on one thing or another. But really, what do I know?'

Hope couldn't help smiling. 'Maybe your mum just likes to involve you?'

'You can say that again,' he said gloomily. 'In everything.'

'It's so exciting,' said Susie. 'We haven't had a big wedding in the village church for a while now.'

'They hold weddings there every other weekend,' said Simon, puzzled.

'Yes, but they're not proper village weddings. Not for someone who has lived here all their lives and who everyone knows. This is going to be special. And with Claire growing up in Midbie she almost counts as local too.'

If Hope remembered correctly, Midbie was less than three miles from St. Ann's Bridge. How close did you have to live to count as local?

'Your parents married in the church,' Susie said reminiscently, turning to Hope. 'You'll have seen the photos?'

Hope frowned. She wasn't sure she had, which was strange. It was all part of her mother not liking to talk about the past. And when she had died Hope had been only too glad to pack up everything and put it into storage, too upset to sort through it. 'I don't remember.'

'I'm sure I've got copies somewhere. I'll look them out for you. I was Maid of Honour, of course. But that was a small wedding compared to the one the Mackenzies are planning.'

'Unfortunately,' said Robbie, still looking gloomy. It was an expression which didn't sit well on his tanned face. So far, Hope had only seen him smiling. 'I suppose I'd better get back. Mamma wanted to talk seating plans and I promised Luke I'd be there to give him some support. Although what he thinks I'll know about it I've no idea.'

'Remind your mum not to put the Gurney family anywhere near Mrs Slater. They haven't spoken since Tommy Gurney ran over her cat in 1979.'

'I'll remind her,' said Robbie as he rose to take his leave.

'You're not serious, are you?' said Hope, amazed.

'Of course I am. In a small community like this feuds run deep and can be very long lasting.'

'Like the secrets,' said Simon, but was silenced by a glare from his wife.

Hope wondered what sort of secrets there could be in this quaint little place. Someone had cheated in the egg and spoon race? Swapped their flowers for an opponent's in the annual fete competition? She couldn't imagine it would be anything worse than that.

Hope's New Job Begins

Robbie didn't know why he was hurrying back to help his brother. Luke hadn't been very supportive during Robbie's latest run-in with their father. But old habits died hard, and the two had always joined forces when Mum was on her high horse. It was the easiest way to survive. Two of them against one of her, diminutive though she was, was just about an even match.

His heart sank when he entered the farm kitchen and found that Claire was also there. She sat next to his mother on one side of the table, as though they were joining forces, so it was two against two.

'There's coffee on the stove,' said his mother, nodding in that direction. 'Help yourself.'

'Thank goodness you're here, I

thought you were never coming.' That was Luke.

'How did Lucy take to being left?' asked Claire, but hardly listened to his answer. She tapped the end of the pen against her lip and said, 'Now, we were just about to start on your family, so it's a good thing you've arrived.'

Robbie met his brother's eyes nervously. Claire's turn of phrase was ominous.

'Get your coffee and come and sit down,' said Luke, sounding as though he personally could have done with something more sustaining than caffeine.

Robbie almost felt sorry for him. He was exchanging his interfering mother and controlling father for a woman who seemed just as keen on organising him, despite her slight frame.

'There are only fifty-three coming from my side of the family, I thought it would be more,' said his mother mournfully. 'Leo and Freddie and their families are coming from Glasgow.'

'Yes, we know who's coming, they're all on the list,' interrupted Robbie quickly. He didn't need yet another rundown of who was and was not attending. And Mum hadn't even started on his father's side of the family, which generally made her even more voluble. 'I thought we were going to talk about seating today? Have you got a copy of the floor plan?'

Claire nodded at him with approval. 'It's here. We're having round tables, as you see, ten at each one. Your mum and I favour mixing people up a bit, my family and yours, but Luke says we should sit people with who they know. What do you think?'

Robbie felt unnerved as three pairs of eyes turned to him. 'Oh, people they know, surely,' he said. 'As long as you're sure they get along.' He remembered Mrs Slater and her poor cat, but decided not to mention that now.

Claire produced another sheet of paper. 'OK, so who shall we put with who?'

49

Robbie tuned out. They really didn't need him here. He was wondering how Lucy was getting on with strangers in her home, and how the girl, Hope, was settling in. Susie Ashbury would no doubt be telling her what to do, but he suspected the girl had backbone and would do what she wanted, when it came to essentials. He liked that idea. That was what he should do, too.

'So what do you think, Robbie?' said his mother, recalling him to the conversation.

'Erm?'

'They want to know if you're bringing a partner,' said Luke helpfully. 'As you haven't got a girlfriend at the moment, unless there's something you aren't telling us, I've assumed you're not. But as Ma's ambition in life is to see us both married off, she's keen that you find someone.'

'I am not keen to have you both married off,' said their mother sternly. 'I only want you to be as happy as your father and I are.'

'Yes, Ma,' said Robbie, rolling his eyes.

Claire put her hand across the table to touch Luke's and at the same time he reached out to her. The way they smiled at each other gave Robbie a jolt. Maybe there was something he was missing out on?

'So, do you want to invite a partner or not?' said his mother.

'I hadn't really thought about it.' Robbie cast his mind over the girls he had been friendly with when he lived at home. As far as he knew, they were now either married or had left the area. For some reason Hope McIlroy came to mind, but he pushed the idea aside. The wedding was weeks away, the girl probably wouldn't even be here by then. 'Who are the bridesmaids? Won't I be busy looking after them?'

Claire giggled. 'My Chief Bridesmaid is my sister, Molly. She'll be seven-months pregnant and has a very protective husband. The flower girls are my twin cousins. They're only ten so they will need looking after if you're willing to take them on?'

'I'm sure there'll be people better qualified than me to do that,' said Robbie quickly. 'Look, do I have to decide about a partner now? The wedding is still ages off and you still haven't had all your replies to the invites.'

'Six weeks off,' said his mother. 'And the deadline for replies is next Friday, so we'll give you until then.'

Robbie wasn't sure whether to be pleased with this respite or not. And how had the wedding got to be so close so quickly? That meant he'd better get a move on with the stag weekend he was (supposedly) arranging for Luke. Why hadn't someone reminded him?

★   ★   ★

Hope was wandering from room to room in Kirkside, anxious to make sure everything was perfect for Mr Jackson's return. She loved the house already and had enjoyed a couple of days here on her own. Now came the big test. Mr Jackson was due to arrive by ambulance in the next half-hour. What would he think of the arrangements she had made? And more importantly, what would he think of her?

Susie had offered to be with her when he arrived, but Hope felt this was something she should do on her own. Besides, Susie's daughter, Sarah, and the grandchildren had arrived so Susie had quite enough to do.

Hope reminded herself she and Mr Jackson seemed to be getting along all right. She had visited him again in the hospital and she thought he liked her company, although he never said so. He was certainly keen enough to see Lucy again.

'He'll be here any minute,' said Hope to the dog who was following her from room to room, as though she knew something was about to happen. 'Not long now,' said Hope, bending to rub the shaggy head. 'In fact, I think that might be them.'

She swallowed hard and went to open the front door, hoping she looked more confident than she felt.

To begin with it was all bustle, the two ambulance men keen to transfer Mr Jackson to the house in their own way and refusing to listen to his insistence he could walk.

'No' up those steps you can't,' said a burly man in his forties, restrapping the belt on the wheelchair.

In a matter of moments the men had transferred Mr Jackson to the house, along with the rather small case containing his possessions.

'Straight into the bed now, is it?' asked one of the men of Hope.

They had already wheeled the chair into the room Hope had indicated as the bedroom. 'Er . . .'

'Definitely not,' said Mr Jackson. He had been ignoring them all, concentrating on greeting Lucy. The dog couldn't bear to be away from his side, giving little bleating noises and rubbing herself against him again and again.

Hope frowned, sure this couldn't be good for her patient, but Mr Jackson didn't seem to mind. 'That's my good leg,' he said, when he saw her staring at him. 'I see they've brought a wheelchair here for me like they said. I suppose you men can help me move over to that and then you can let me be. Can't you see I want to look around my house, not be put straight into yet another bed?'

The men looked doubtfully at Hope. 'If you could help Mr Jackson into the other chair that would be very kind,' she said, adding in an undertone, 'I think there's a nurse coming around later, she'll help him into bed.'

'Nurses, bah! I've had enough of them and all,' said Mr Jackson, proving he wasn't nearly as hard of hearing as he claimed.

All too quickly the ambulance men had completed their tasks and driven away. Hope and Mr Jackson were left alone in the house.

'Would you, er, like some tea?' she

asked hesitantly. What on earth was she supposed to do? She didn't even know this man. She could quite see why he wouldn't want her in his home, and yet it was her job to look after him.

'Not just now,' he said. 'I'm going to look around.' He began to move the wheelchair experimentally and banged the door frame as he turned. 'I could walk fine, you know, but I'm a wee bit tired.'

'Would you like me to help?'

'No, I wouldn't. Leave me alone. Haven't you got something else you can do?' He manoeuvred the chair through the doorway, bumping it again with one of the back wheels. 'Stupid thing! There, Lucy, that's right, you show me what's been going on here.'

Hope watched as he turned the chair, just managing to miss the door frame. She wished she'd thought to remove some of the furniture, there wouldn't be much room for the wheelchair in there.

She waited to see if he would call her, but he didn't. He pushed the door closed and she heard him moving about, and all the while he was speaking to his darling dog.

He was fine. She went to sit in the kitchen and wait until she was wanted.

She had prepared a simple lunch of salad and cold meats. She's asked Mr Jackson if he wanted anything in particular, but he had said he didn't mind, as long as it didn't come on a plastic hospital tray. Hope felt she could guarantee that, at least.

In the early afternoon the nurse arrived and then Mr Jackson agreed to go for a lie down. Hope began to relax a little. She had seen he was quite mobile and wouldn't need as much help as she had feared. The nurse left Hope a leaflet explaining what Mr Jackson should or shouldn't do, and she settled down to read it.

Apparently sitting or lying for any period of time was not a good idea. He had been given a set of exercises by the hospital physiotherapist. Hope looked over the list and when Mr Jackson rose from his nap she set about encouraging him to try them.

'Not just now, lass,' he said, when she first made the suggestion.

Hope decided to wait until after he had had his afternoon tea, then she tried again. 'The nurse and the physio were both saying how important it is for you to move around. Why don't you just try . . . '

Mr Jackson banged his hand on the table, making his cup and saucer rattle. 'Leave me be! Can't I make up my own mind what I want to do in my own house? I've been nagged to death for weeks now. You just leave me be.'

He manoeuvred the wheelchair out of the kitchen, leaving his tea unfinished.

Hope sat there on her own for a while. She found she was shaking.

She was only trying to do her best. After a while she went up to her room and tried to distract herself with a book. Mr Jackson was tired, that was why he was so irritable. Things would be better tomorrow, really they would.

Hope Confides In Robbie

To Hope's relief, Mr Jackson's temper improved slightly over the next few days. He even patted her hand one evening and told her not to mind him when he was grumpy. But he was still reluctant to do the exercises, and only picked at the food Hope prepared. He seemed more interested in Lucy than in people.

Hope found she was starting to feel lonely, which was ridiculous. Susie and her daughter and grandchildren had popped in and invited her out with them, but she felt she couldn't leave Mr Jackson for too long.

She was more delighted than she should have been by the appearance of Robbie Mackenzie late one afternoon. Many of the villagers had, of course, come to see how Mr Jackson was and had chatted politely to Hope, but this was different. This was someone she almost knew.

'He's a bit grumpy today, isn't he?' said Robbie cheerfully when he joined Hope in the kitchen after spending time with Mr Jackson and Lucy.

'He's still in quite a lot of pain,' said Hope, immediately keen to defend her charge.

'Didn't the hospital give him something for that?'

'Yes.' Hope pushed her long hair back and sighed. 'But he won't take it as often as he needs. Says he's had enough pills to last him a lifetime and he'd rather feel what he's meant to feel.'

'He's a tough old stick.'

'Yes.' Hope smiled. Despite everything, she was growing to respect the old man. 'He certainly is.'

'What have you been doing?' asked Robbie, looking around the old-fashioned kitchen. 'I'm sure the deal wasn't that you would spend all your days slaving away in here.'

'Of course not. I've just put a

casserole on for supper.' Hope took the cups off the tray which Robbie had carried through. 'I'll tidy these away and then I'm free for a while. Mr Jackson is very good about it, in fact I think he's keen to get me out of the house, but I feel worried if I leave him alone too long.'

'A walk up to the farm wouldn't take too long, would it?' Robbie smiled encouragingly. He had beautiful dark eyes that sparkled as though this was an excellent idea.

'I don't know . . . '

'Come on. My mum is worried about you here on your own so much, she'd love to see you.'

Hope felt disappointed it was Robbie's mother who wanted to see her, but at least that made it easier to agree. 'All right. As long as it's OK with Mr Jackson.'

Robbie grinned again. 'It is. I already asked him.' For the second time in a few minutes Hope's spirits lifted. Perhaps he really did want to spend time with her? In any case, it would be good to get out of the house.

'We'll take the scenic route,' said Robbie, turning left out of Kirkside's drive. As far as Hope knew, this led only to the church, but she followed obediently. They walked past the old stone wall that surrounded the church-yard, across the rough parking area and down to the river. Hope had never thought to push her way through the long grass and brambles, but Robbie seemed to know what he was doing.

'There used to be a path here somewhere ... Aye, here it is.' He stamped down the grass to make it easier for her to reach him and held out a hand when she almost overbalanced avoiding a bramble that seemed deter-mined to cling on to her skirt. She didn't really need his help, but it was kind of him to worry. He continued to hold her hand for a moment as he drew her to the water's edge and she was sorry when he let go.

'It's lovely down here,' she said.

There were willows overhanging the slow-moving water and the banks on both sides were overgrown with nettles and reeds and masses of wild flowers.

'The water's low at this time of year. In winter it can be a torrent. It's a good river, though, not very polluted and I hear the salmon are better than ever this year.'

Hope looked around with new eyes. She had heard from Susie that Robbie worked as some kind of countryside warden. He would know about things like that. To him the river was more than just a pretty sight.

'It doesn't look like pollution was ever a problem here.'

'Oh, believe me, it has been. There used to be a small animal-feed factory upstream which was forever discharging waste into the burn that fed into the Kinnen Water here. If you have too many nutrients you upset the whole ecological balance. And more recently there have been problems with silage run-off. Not from our farm, we don't have silage, and I have to say Dad is very particular about not causing pollution. Unfortunately, there are others who just don't care.'

'Gosh,' said Hope, realising how little she knew about country life.

'Sorry, I shouldn't bore you. Come on, I'll show you where this path goes and I promise, no more lectures.'

'You weren't lecturing.' Hope hurried after him along the narrow path, pulling her skirts in to avoid thistles. They came to a fence which must mark the beginning of the Mackenzies' farm. A hessian sack had been fastened over the barbed wire to make it easier to climb. At least, it was easier for Robbie with his long legs and old jeans. Hope looked down doubtfully at her crushed velvet skirt with lace petticoat peeping beneath. It really wasn't ideal for country walks.

'I'm not sure . . . '

'Gather all the loose fabric in one hand and step over. You'll be fine, and if you're not, I'll catch you.'

Hope didn't want to seem useless, so she did as instructed. It wasn't easy, but somehow she managed to get over.

'I really should look into finding some more practical clothes.'

'No, don't. I've never seen anyone wear things like you do. They're amazing.'

'Why . . . thanks.' Hope was unreasonably pleased. She thought he had hardly noticed her, never mind the clothes she wore. 'I make most of them myself. At first it was just to save money, but then I found I really loved it.' She stopped. He wouldn't be interested in that.

Robbie smiled across at her. They were now in a field and there was room for them to walk side by side.

'Didn't Susie Ashbury say something about you having your own fabric shop? That must have been fun.'

Hope waited for the familiar cloud of despair to descend. It did, but this time it wasn't quite so bad. Maybe Susie was right, putting some distance between herself and the disaster was helping.

'It had to close down,' she said softly. 'I loved that place and I thought we could make something of it, but . . . it didn't work out.'

'What happened?' Robbie seemed genuinely interested, sympathetic rather than judgemental.

'I made a mistake with the business partner I chose.' She swallowed, hoping this wasn't going to make her cry. It was still so hard to talk about what had gone wrong. 'A big mistake. Amy and I were at college together and she was fun, a little crazy, but with so many fantastic ideas, I thought we would be an ideal partnership. I was the more down to earth one and she was . . . ' Hope thought of the pleasure they had had in the first months of their new business. She had been desperate to keep herself busy, still reeling from the loss of her mother a year earlier.

Amy had insisted they 'think big' and take on larger premises and more stock than Hope had wanted. But there was no one else to advise them and at first things seemed to go well. Maybe it would have continued to do so, if Amy hadn't let her down.

'She was?' prompted Robbie.

Hope stopped suddenly, with the grass brushing her bare legs and the breeze blowing through her hair. She took a deep breath. It was the first time she had said this out loud. 'She was a liar and a crook.' And then as soon as she said it she felt bad. 'I don't think she meant to behave like she did, maybe she didn't even see it as dishonesty . . . '

It had started with Amy taking stock out of the business for her own use and not paying. Hope had suspected this but hadn't known how to challenge her friend. Then it had moved on to her selling stock privately and keeping the money for herself. Hope had only found out about this later. And then, worst of all, Amy had emptied the till, taken what was left in the joint bank account, and simply disappeared.

'I was left with nothing,' Hope said slowly, shaking her head as she remembered the shock of finding no money at all, and no Amy. 'I should have suspected, but I didn't.'

Robbie pulled her into a hug. 'Don't look like that. You're not responsible for someone else's dishonesty.'

It felt good to be held by him, even though Hope was unable to believe his words. 'I should have known,' she said. 'I put half the money my mother left me into that business. I should have been more careful.'

And it wasn't just her dream she had lost, she had also let down so many other people. The accountant was still trying to work out how much money was owed.

'You poor thing,' said Robbie, giving her another hug and keeping hold of her hand as they began to walk on. 'It must have been awful. So you came up here to make a new start?'

'I came up here because Aunt Susie suggested it. She seemed to think it was a good idea. And I didn't know what else to do.'

'Well I for one am very glad you came.'

Hope blushed. She extricated her hand from his as they entered the farm yard. All the same, his words brought a warm, happy feeling to her she hadn't known for a long time.

The visit to Holm Farm was fun, and not just because of that walk through the fields with Robbie. It was a chance to get to know his exuberant mother a little better and to meet his brother and father.

His father was a taciturn man with greying ginger hair who only popped in for a short while. His brother, Luke, was a shorter, stockier version of Robbie. He came in as they were drinking their coffee and began raiding the cake tins.

'You see what I have to put up with?' said Maria Mackenzie happily. 'No matter how often I bake, those tins never seem to stay full.'

'You shouldn't make such delicious things, then we wouldn't be forced to eat them,' said Robbie, helping himself to a second scone.

'I don't see anyone forcing you.'

'We need to keep our strength up,' said Luke, spreading butter lavishly over a slice of fruit loaf. 'You wouldn't want us to fade away.'

Maria looked fondly at both her boys. Hope wondered what it was like to be part of such a busy, happy family.

She smiled to herself all the way home. They were so funny, with their teasing and their plans, but what she liked most of all was their obvious affection for each other. She hoped she would see more of the Mackenzies during her stay.

★   ★   ★

Hope's life was settling down into a routine. She rose early each day, let Lucy out into the garden and helped Mr Jackson to get ready. Then she made tea for them both and they waited for the first visit from the district nurse. After that came breakfast and any cleaning chores she could manage to do without Mr Jackson being aware of them. He didn't see why she should do any of them when he had a cleaner coming in twice a week, but Hope felt she needed to earn her pay.

Susie had thought she would be good company for Mr Jackson, but he liked to keep to himself. He had enough talking with all the visitors who called by, he didn't need any more jollying along from Hope.

She could see that he was finding it very tiring being at home. She was rather pleased with herself for managing to persuade him to take a rest each afternoon.

'I don't need to rest, ridiculous idea,' he had said after the first couple of days.

'I know you don't need to. But if I told people that you had a little lie down every day after lunch, that would stop them calling in to see you?'

He eyed her thoughtfully. His face was more gaunt than ever. He really did need to rest. She was sure he wasn't sleeping well, but he wouldn't admit it. 'That's not a bad idea,' he said at last. 'Folk in this village would kill you with kindness.'

And so it was agreed she would fend off visitors in the afternoons. Mr Jackson retired to his room to lie on the bed.

One afternoon at the end of the second week, she found herself at a loose end. The evening meal was already prepared. She didn't like to leave the house in case Mr Jackson woke. And then the phone rang. It was Tommy Grainger, the accountant in charge of liquidating her shop, *Material Things*.

Hope's good mood evaporated. Tommy was a nice enough man, always pleasant when Hope had dealings with him, but he was in charge of winding up her lovely business. Every time she spoke to him she was reminded of her failure, and that it didn't just affect her but all those people she owed money to as well. Perhaps he had finally worked out what all the debts of the partnership were.

'I think we've managed to wind everything up now. I'm fairly confident I have got hold of all the outstanding paperwork,' he said.

'That's good.' Hope held her breath, waiting to hear how bad the situation was.

He named an amount that was large, but actually not as bad as she had feared. 'That's the total of your creditors. Now, I can try to come to a voluntary arrangement with them, but I fear we may have to formally liquidate the partnership. That way they take any assets that are left, but can't touch anything that belongs to you — or Miss Amy Jones, if she ever reappears. It's lucky you set up a limited liability partnership.'

Hope took his word for that, she didn't really understand these things.

'So there will definitely be people whose bills won't be paid?'

'I'm afraid so. Also, if the business is liquidated, it will make it difficult for you to ever start a business again, which is something you might want to consider.'

'I'm not thinking of starting a business again,' said Hope with a wry smile. 'But I'm not prepared to have all those people who supplied us and supported us go without their money. I can afford the amount you said. I'll pay them myself.'

'But you can't do that!' The man sounded horrified. 'The whole point of limited liability is that you don't have to lose everything you have. Really, Hope, I wouldn't advise this.'

'I won't lose everything,' said Hope brightly. She would be left with a few thousand pounds, which was more than many people had, wasn't it? Tommy Grainger tried to talk her out of it, but she insisted.

When the conversation ended, she

felt unreasonably cheered. She had made the right decision, of that she was sure.

She went up to her room, leaving the door open in case Mr Jackson called, and almost without thinking she lifted her sewing machine onto the table and took off its case. She ran her hand over the creamy surface and realised it was dusty. That needed seeing to. The machine had been her twenty-first birthday present, not long before her mother died. It was a little gem. It didn't deserve to be neglected.

After she had polished it, she pulled out the material samples that had lain in the bottom of her suitcase. She certainly wasn't short of material. All the unsold roll-ends from the shop had fallen to her. Most of them were still in storage in Brighton, but despite everything she hadn't been able to travel without a few bits and pieces.

She fingered the pale blue ruched cotton. It wasn't something she was likely to wear herself but it would make a lovely dress for Susie's six-year-old granddaughter, Megan. She hadn't been able to do much for Susie to thank her for all her help. Why not? She began to page through her book of patterns. She could make a start now and do a proper fitting when she next saw the child.

Within minutes she was lost to the world. It was so wonderful! Should she do a high bodice or a low waist? Long sleeves or short? A little broderie anglaise fitted in at the neck would be perfect for a little girl who loved pretty things. This was such fun!

* * *

The next afternoon she intended to get straight back to her sewing, but was disturbed by Susie herself. Her god-mother phoned just before lunch to see if Hope wanted to go for a walk.

Hope wondered why. Susie didn't normally go for walks.

'Aren't Sarah and the children with

you?' she asked as they set out.

'No. They've gone to spend the day with a school-friend of Sarah's. It'll be a nice change for them and I thought it would give me a chance to see you. I feel I've been neglecting you since they arrived.'

'Of course you haven't! It's been fun to meet Sarah again, but mostly I've been busy with Mr Jackson. He's not hard work, but I don't like to leave him too long.' Hope worried he would try to do too much if she wasn't there to stop him.

'We're not going far. I just wanted to show you Cleughbrae . . . and here we are.'

They had once again followed the winding road away from the village and had now come to a stop at the head of the dark track Susie had pointed out a couple of weeks before. Hope had considered going to look at the house herself, but something held her back.

'Why do you want to show me?'

'Aren't you interested?'

'Well, yes.' Hope was also uneasy. Susie seemed so serious, unlike her normal self.

She turned and led the way down beneath the trees. It was quieter here and smelt of damp soil and leaves. Despite the warm summer, nothing seemed to have dried out.

The track sloped towards the river, veering to the right. It became rougher. Water rivulets had cut their way through the soil and no one had bothered to make repairs. Susie's silence was beginning to weigh on Hope.

Eventually they emerged into a small clearing with a tumbledown red-sandstone cottage in the centre. The grass around it had been roughly cut and there were curtains at the windows, so Hope presumed the place was lived in, yet it had a forlorn air, as though unloved. She looked at it for a long time.

'It's, er, not what I expected,' she said at last. She really couldn't picture her neat and tidy mother growing up here.

'It didn't used to be like this,' said Susie, peering around. 'The local estate bought it when your grandmother died and they've been using it to house various workers. No one seems to stay here long. They don't seem to have taken much care of it.'

They began to walk around.

'Is there anyone in it now?' said Hope. 'Will they mind us being so nosy?'

'The family, who were here moved out last month. No one will mind. It's a pity I didn't ask for the key, actually, and you could have had a look inside.'

Hope wasn't sure she would have wanted to look inside. The place was depressing. On the northern side the stone was stained green. The windows were unwashed and paint was peeling from the frames. It was small. When they peered through the windows the rooms looked cramped. With the trees gathering so close around it would be dark inside, and almost certainly damp.

'I can't picture my mum here,' she said.

'It was different then,' said Susie. 'They used to have hens around the back here. And a vegetable garden, yes, look you can see where it was. Your grandfather was a keen gardener.'

'He was?' Hope peered at the faint evidence of raised beds at the side of the house, now covered in grass and weeds. She tried to picture her mother here, an adopted child of elderly parents, and failed.

'Yes. He was a lovely man, your grandfather. He never quite recovered from what happened to him in the war, the Second World War, you know? He was missing-presumed-dead for many years. It turned out he was in a prisoner-of-war camp. That was a difficult time for your grandmother. Did you know they hadn't been married long when he went off to the war? When she thought she'd lost him she moved to Glasgow to do war work there.'

'That must have been awful.' Hope had never heard any of this. She looked around at the funny little house once again, beginning to feel a connection. This was where her family had lived — except, of course, that it wasn't. Her mother was adopted, so there was no blood connection.

'Yes, it must have been a very difficult time for Jane.'

'Jane?'

'Jane Elspeth Calvert, nee Irving. Your grandmother. Your mother was named after her.'

Hope frowned. This didn't seem right. 'But how could that be? I thought Mum was adopted when she was three. Did they change her name then? That would be so confusing for a child . . . '

'No, they didn't change her name. She had always been Elspeth.' Susie sighed. 'I wanted your mother to tell you but she didn't, did she?'

'No. Tell me what?' Even as Hope asked the question, she wasn't sure she wanted to know.

Susie took a deep breath. 'Your mother wasn't adopted at all. At least she was, officially, but Jane and Joseph were also her biological parents.'

'They were . . . what?' Hope's words sounded faint even to her. What had Susie said? It didn't make sense.

Susie put a hand on her arm. 'Your mother's adoptive parents were also her real parents. Your real grandparents.'

Hope could feel her heart beating loudly in her chest. She felt as though she had been winded. This changed everything she had grown up believing.

Her mother wasn't adopted. She hadn't been a cuckoo in the nest, never quite fitting in, never happy in this strange family.

'And my mother knew this?' she said slowly.

'Yes, she did — eventually. Come and sit down over here and I'll tell you about it.'

Susie led the way to a rusting garden bench and, after brushing off the twigs and leaves, they sat down. Hope felt dizzy. Everything was different. With an effort she forced herself to concentrate on what Susie was telling her.

'It's not that unusual a story, in some ways,' said Susie softly. 'Jane and Joseph were both in their thirties when they got married, I'm not exactly sure why they left it so late. And then not long after the marriage he went off to war. What they didn't know was that Jane was expecting his child at the time.

'Well, you can imagine how awful it was for Jane when his family received the telegram telling them he was missing-presumed-dead. We don't know any of the details, but we do know she took herself off to Glasgow soon after that. You have to remember that bringing up a child on your own wasn't like it is today. It would have been a real struggle. It seems that Jane had the child and then gave her up. She would have thought she was doing the best thing for the child. Jane must have kept in touch with her, but as far as we know she still told no one about her baby.'

Hope shook her head, trying to take all this in. 'And then her fiancé came back? What a shock that must have been.'

'Yes. A wonderful one in many ways. And when he learnt of the child's existence they were determined to get her back. Your mother was officially adopted by them. The problem was, they didn't tell anyone in St. Ann's Bridge the truth. The stigma of a mother giving up her child must have been terrible, at least in Jane and Joseph's eyes. So they brought up their own daughter, and they loved her, I can assure you of that. What they didn't realise was that your mother had her own stigma to deal with, the teasing about being adopted, the believing she didn't belong. It was very hard for her.'

'But they did tell her, eventually?' said Hope. 'You said she did know.'

'Yes. Your grandfather died the year your mother and I started our nursing training. Your mother missed him terribly. I told you, he was a lovely man.

Your grandmother was different, she could be very hard.' Susie sighed again. 'I'm sure she was only trying to do what was right, in her eyes. Anyway, soon after the funeral, for some reason she told your mother the truth. I think she wanted your mother to realise how much she, Jane, had suffered. But Elspeth didn't see it that way. I think it nearly broke her heart, to know she had been brought up with such a lie.'

Hope was silent, trying to take all this in. She had heard of children being brought up as one of the family and finding out later they were adopted. She had never heard of a story like this one. It was so weird.

'But why? It all seems so silly. Why not tell the truth?'

'Things were different then.'

'So why didn't Mum tell me the truth, at least? I don't understand.'

'I think she found it hard to accept,' said Susie gently. 'I tried to persuade her to tell you, but she said she'd been brought up to believe she wasn't truly a

Calvert and that was the way she felt. She felt adopted.'

'Poor Mum,' said Hope. But after the initial sympathy, she also felt anger. This made a difference to her, too. All the things she could have known but didn't. All the things she had missed out on.

She looked around again. 'So this is where my grandparents lived? My real grandparents.'

'That's right,' said Susie, giving her a hug. 'I'm so glad you know the truth.' She seemed relieved. 'Now, if you don't want to be away from Kirkside too long perhaps we should be getting back? We'll have plenty of time to talk more about this later.'

Hope followed her up the gloomy track in a daze. It was going to take a long time to sort this out in her head. Suddenly, everything she had thought was true had shifted, as though the world had tipped on its side.

★　★　★

86

Hope couldn't get the things Susie had told her out of her head. Her mother had been brought up thinking she was adopted — but actually she wasn't. How could her mother have known all this and said nothing to her?

Mr Jackson noticed something was wrong as soon as she returned from the walk to Cleughbrae. 'You all right, lass? What has Susie Ashbury been doing to you?'

Hope tried to shrug his comments off. It was her problem. But her thoughts grew more and more confused. By the following evening, she needed to talk. When they sat down to eat their evening meal she found herself blurting out, 'Susie told me about my mother, about her growing up at Cleughbrae.'

'Aye, I mind Elspeth Calvert. She was a quiet wee thing. Shame about all that adoption malarkey.'

'But the thing was, she wasn't adopted.' It was the first time Hope had said these words out loud.

'Aye, I know.'

'You know?' Hope stared at him, stunned all over again. How could he know this, her family's dark secret?

'Once Jane Calvert started telling people about it you couldn't shut her up. It fair took us by surprise to begin with, but they were aye ones for keeping secrets, the Irving family.'

'The Irving family?' said Hope, confused.

'Jane was an Irving, didn't you know? It was Joseph's family, the Calverts, who were brought up at Cleughbrae. Five boys there were, if I mind right, and Joseph the youngest. The Irvings lived in one of those cottages near the school and they liked to keep themselves to themselves, for all they lived in the middle of the village. Of course, Jane's father was dead by the time it all came out. I know what he would have made of it.'

Hope swallowed hard. Suddenly, she felt she wanted to cry. He was talking about her family. Mr Jackson actually knew and remembered them, knew things about them and about her she was only just learning. From what he said, it sounded like the whole village knew. She felt quite ill. It wasn't right. Why hadn't anybody told her sooner?

Mr Jackson obviously expected her to ask more questions. But now she found she didn't want to know. She hastened to finish her meal and clear away so she could retreat to the sanctuary of her bedroom. This second revelation, that the whole village knew her secret before she did, was almost harder to come to terms with than the first one.

★ ★ ★

Hope didn't sleep well in the nights following her conversations with Susie and then Mr Jackson. She managed to get through the days, more or less. She avoided Susie by saying Mr Jackson had taken a turn for the worse. It was partly true, he was certainly very tired. She avoided talking to Mr Jackson by simply ignoring it every time he made reference to her family. And she kept away from the villagers. Even the Mackenzies no longer seemed the open friendly family she had admired. They had all known and no one had said anything.

She couldn't stop thinking, though. She rose early one Sunday morning and decided to take a walk down to the graveyard. From Mr Jackson's words she assumed this was where her grandparents were buried. She couldn't yet bear to return to Cleughbrae, but she wanted to do something. Maybe this would help sort out her jumbled thoughts.

She obtained Mr Jackson's permission to take Lucy with her and set off down to the old graveyard down by the river.

Nobody had been buried here for many years, but the grass underfoot was kept reasonably short and the pathways weeded. Hope wandered along them in the cool early morning, wondering what on earth she was looking for. There were so many gravestones, all the same dark red sandstone, but in varying degrees of decay. Some were so covered with lichen or leant at such a drunken angle she couldn't read the words. Others were still upright and perfectly legible.

Without realising it, she found herself drawn in. Once you read one stone you couldn't resist thinking about those long ago people, and then moving on to the next to find out more.

There were certain family names that cropped up again and again. *Thorburn* and *Mackenzie* and *Angus* were very common.

And then, all of a sudden, she found the one she was looking for. *Calvert. Joseph Calvert.* Her mouth went dry as she stood before it and slowly read the inscription.

In loving memory of Joseph Calvert who died at Cleughbrae 10th Sept 1963 aged 58 years. Also Jane Irving Calvert, his wife, who died at Cleughbrae 30th January 1983 aged 77 years.

THY WILL BE DONE.

At the top of the gravestone were two carved stone flowers. Otherwise it was plain and very moving in its simplicity. Hope stared at it for a long time. In loving memory. In loving memory. Joseph Calvert had been loved. What about Jane? Somehow she thought Jane was less loveable and yet she was the one who had chosen those words, she had loved Joseph.

Hope turned away. It was time to take Lucy home.

As she left the graveyard she saw a figure in the neighbouring field. He raised his hand in greeting and she realised it was Robbie Mackenzie, now approaching the fence to say hello. It was surprisingly good to see Robbie again, to chat casually about this and that. He was very easy to talk to. He told her about the stag weekend he was arranging for his brother and how, when it was over, he was looking forward to doing some work on the upland bogs.

Hope had no idea what 'upland bogs' were, but was flattered he wanted to discuss them with her. As she headed back to Kirkside she found herself thinking of Robbie and not her family problems, and feeling far more cheerful.

★   ★   ★

Robbie really wasn't looking forward to the stag weekend. Nine young men were going to camp at Knockencraig Bothy, which meant an awful lot of food and drink to organise.

At least they were all sorting out their own bedding and, as the building only took six, Callum had said he'd bring along a tent. They were to meet up at Johnnie Macmillan's place, the nearest to the start of the path, at midday on Saturday. Robbie would then distribute the food and drink between them and they would set off.

The weather was looking promising. Maybe it wasn't going to be too bad.

'Thank goodness we got away,' said Luke as they pulled out of St. Ann's Bridge and headed west. 'I thought Dad was never going to finish with things he needed us to do.'

'Or Claire with suggestions about what you should and shouldn't take,' said Robbie with a grin. 'Lucky mobiles don't work up there or she'd be checking up on you all night.'

Luke just smiled. He didn't seem to mind.

The walk from the Macmillan's farm to Knockencraig normally took about four hours but, with their extra load, they had allowed five. This would mean arriving late afternoon which left plenty of time to put up the tent, build a fire, and generally get themselves sorted for a long lazy evening.

The bothy was set on the banks of a lochan, just off the Southern Upland Way. It was a beautiful location, with the dark cliff of the Capple Craig to the rear and the hills rising all around. The rampant growth of grass and bracken in the summer was already starting to die back, giving hints of yellow and brown to the vibrant green Robbie had been enjoying so much. But every season was different, and all had something to treasure.

'Phew, glad I didn't remember how far this was or I wouldn't have agreed to come,' said Callum as they arrived on the patch of flattened grass in front of the bothy.

'You townies need to get a bit fitter,' said Luke, tossing aside his own pack. It was true he had carried more than anyone except Robbie, and not struggled at all.

'Going to those gyms isn't nearly as good for you as some honest farm work,' agreed Johnnie Macmillan, who worked with his father on their family farm.

'Nothing wrong with being a townie,' said Chris. He now lived in Edinburgh where he worked as a solicitor. He was a tall very thin man who was only now growing out of his teenage gangliness. 'I bet I could get up those cliffs twice as quick as the rest of you.'

'Bet you couldn't,' said Luke, eyeing them with interest. As a boy he'd always been the one most likely to climb on the hay ricks or the barn roofs — and then fall off, ending up in Accident and Emergency.

'Hey, we're here for food, drink and the views,' said Robbie quickly. 'We haven't any kit to go climbing.'

'Who said anything about kit?' said Chris, waving languidly towards the dark rock. 'Don't you know the big thing now is free climbing? I've tried it at Ratho a few times. The adrenaline kick you get is awesome.'

'Let's get the fire going, shall we?' said Robbie, keen to change the subject. He didn't want them to start doing anything stupid. His father had made it quite clear whose fault it would be if Luke didn't arrive back in one piece.

Fortunately, once they had started eating the food, climbing seemed to be forgotten. The guys were more Luke's friends than Robbie's, but he knew them well enough to join in the teasing and catch up on the gossip about mutual acquaintances. The lengthy discussions about football left him cold, but you couldn't have everything.

Whilst they argued about Queens' chances of promotion in the coming season, his mind drifted to how different it was up here with so many people around. To be honest, he preferred it when he was on his own. Luke's friends were a good crowd, but they were rowdy.

Robbie wondered what it would be like to bring Hope McIlroy. She was the very opposite of rowdy. He thought, somehow, she would enjoy the tranquil beauty of the place. He smiled at the thought of her drifting along in the twilight in those strange floaty clothes of hers. Maybe not the most practical for the climb up here, though.

The evening was, amazingly, a great success. They all drank a little too much, especially Luke, who was egged on to try whisky chasers after his beers. But they were tired after the long hike and, to Robbie's vast relief, turned in not long after midnight.

★ ★ ★

After a good night's sleep, the crowd were in high spirits again, helped no doubt by the vast breakfast Robbie found himself cooking for everyone. His mother had insisted he take all the ingredients as she was sure a proper breakfast would be appreciated. It was, but it was also hard work! Maybe he should appreciate his mother more?

'What are we going to do this morning?' said Luke. 'We don't need to head back until eleven-ish. Who's up for walking to the top of Nether Coomb?' He gestured to the nearest of the hills, showing mistily in the morning sun-shine.

'I vote for climbing Capple Craig,' said Chris. 'I don't know when I'll next be here and it looks a great wee cliff.'

'I'm not really sure we have time for either,' said Robbie. 'It'll take a while to clear up.' As a countryside ranger he was determined to leave the bothy in a pristine state.

'I'm keen to have a shot at the cliff,' said Chris, ignoring Robbie. He waved his long-fingered hand towards it. 'Who's up for a shot?'

'I'll give it a go,' said Luke immediately.

'I've no head for heights,' said Callum. 'I'll pack up the tent and help Robbie with the tidying.'

'Hey, who said I was in charge of tidying?' But Robbie found himself losing the argument. Freddie and the Smith brothers said they'd brought their rods and wanted to try some fishing. The rest were determined to give the cliff a go, or at least watch Chris attempt it.

'Look, don't do anything stupid, OK?' said Robbie as they set off.

At least he could see them from here.

They wouldn't even be out of earshot. There wasn't much time, an hour at the most, and then he would shout them to come back and they would set off home. He was looking forward to getting back. Being the only responsible one amongst nine men was proving more of a strain than he had expected.

The packing was almost finished when Robbie's attention was drawn to the cliffs. Callum yelled, 'Crikey! What on earth . . . ?'

Robbie ran out of the house, almost hitting his head on the low lintel, and turned to look up the hillside. Three figures were strung out across the face of the cliffs, a good thirty metres from the ground. The first he could identify as Chris from the red hair and slim build. The second, he saw with mounting panic, had to be Luke. He would recognise him anywhere and, besides, no-one else was wearing a green tee-shirt. He wasn't sure who the third figure was, but that one was not so high and already retreating.

He could hear the sound of their voices carried by the wind, but not their actual words.

'I think they're stuck,' said Callum.

'Chris isn't. He's carrying on. But Luke . . . '

There was something wrong with the way Luke was moving, or not moving. He seemed to be hunched against the dark face of the rock, frozen.

Robbie began to run. Luke was a fool. Why had he gone up so high? Why could he never resist a challenge? He was almost there, his lungs pumping from the effort, when it happened.

He heard Luke's muffled words of, 'I can't . . . ' and then one foot slipped and he lost his hand-hold. He tumbled in what seemed like slow motion down the face of the crag, bouncing off it at one point, coming to rest in a sickening heap on the short grass at the foot.

Robbie Makes A Sacrifice

Susie appeared at Kirkside after church. Hope was still trying to avoid her, but for once Susie wasn't interested in her goddaughter.

'I thought you'd like to know,' she said breathlessly to Hope and Mr Jackson who were both in the kitchen. 'I've just heard. One of the Mackenzie boys has been badly injured, they're taking him straight to hospital.'

Hope looked at her in horror.

Mr Jackson said, 'Been hurt on the farm, like? That'll be Luke then.'

'No, not on the farm. They were away up in the hills for the weekend and something has happened. I'm not sure what. I think they've had to get Mountain Rescue out. Simon has gone round to see Maria now, to see if there is anything we can do. I'd better catch up with him.'

Don't let it be Robbie, thought Hope, and then felt guilty. Just because she didn't know Luke didn't make it any better if he was hurt. But she had liked Robbie, and the thought of him injured made her feel quite sick. He knew the hills so well, surely it couldn't be him.

'What happened?' she asked, but Susie was already on her way out.

'I hope it's not serious,' said Mr Jackson lugubriously. 'They young lads don't think when they go off gallivanting. Lucky we didn't have time for that kind of thing in my day.'

'It was Luke's stag weekend,' said Hope, remembering. 'He's supposed to get married next month. Gosh, I wonder if Claire has heard what's happened.'

She wished there was something she could do, but there wasn't. She hardly knew the slight, blonde girl who was Luke's fiancée. There would be people far more useful than her to rally around Maria Mackenzie and her husband. All

Hope could do was wait. At least this had taken her mind off her own problems.

* * *

Robbie travelled in the back of the ambulance with Luke. The last couple of hours were a blur, seeing Luke fall, trying to find out how badly he was hurt, waiting for Mountain Rescue, and then hurry down the hill beside them.

'I don't think it's as bad as it looks,' one of them had said. 'He's not lost consciousness again. He's making a fuss. That's a good sign.'

Robbie was pretty sure his brother had a broken leg. He also had hundreds of cuts and bruises. But as long as that was all, as long as there was no internal damage or injury to his head . . . Robbie shivered despite the warmth inside the vehicle. His mother and Claire were meeting him at Dumfries Hospital. He really didn't know what he was going to say to them.

It seemed like hours later when the three of them were sitting in the canteen.

'I can't believe he was so stupid,' said Claire for the twentieth time.

'He always did like to climb,' said his mother.

'I should have stopped him,' said Robbie.

'It's not your fault,' said Claire. He was grateful for her words. He doubted his father would be so understanding.

Claire took a sip of her coffee and gave a long sigh of relief. 'Now he's out of theatre and back on the ward and we know the only real damage is the broken leg — well, it's not the end of the world, is it?'

'But you're getting married in three weeks' time,' wailed Maria. Once she knew her son's life wasn't in danger she had transferred her worries to the wedding. 'Everything's booked, it's all organised. Whatever are we going to do?'

It was Claire who said, 'He can get

married with a broken leg, you know.' Robbie had thought this too, but it sounded better coming from her. 'He and I'll need to talk about it when he's in a fit state to do so, but I don't think it should be a problem.'

'You mean you still want to marry him, even if he is an idiot?' asked Robbie.

'Of course.' Claire smiled. 'But that doesn't mean I'm not going to give him a piece of my mind, first.'

'And me,' said Maria with feeling. 'And that will be nothing to what his father will have to say. In fact, here he is. He can tell us exactly what he thinks of his oldest son.'

Maria hurried off to help her husband choose from the self-service counter, as if he couldn't manage on his own. But all too soon they were back at the table. Once his father had been filled in on Luke's condition he turned on Robbie. 'What on earth did you let him do that for?' His tone was grim, his expression stony. 'I told you it was a foolish idea, going off for the night like that.'

'It's not Robbie's fault,' protested Maria.

'I'll speak to Luke when I see him. But you, boy, what were you thinking of? You know your brother only has to step on to a wall to fall off it. Why on earth didn't you stop him?'

Robbie looked at the blazing anger in his father's face and remembered all the other times he'd been in the wrong, how nothing he ever did seemed to be right. This time, for once, he agreed with his father.

'I'm sorry,' he said. He still felt sick when he thought of Luke's body lying at the foot of the cliff. It was his fault. 'It was — pretty awful for a bit, when we didn't know how badly he was hurt . . . '

'Don't talk about that,' said Claire quickly.

'What I want to know is, how am I going to manage on the farm?' continued his father. 'Sounds like the boy will be no use to anyone for weeks. This might not be the busiest time of year, but there's still too much to do for one man. 'I don't know . . . '

For a few moments Robbie tuned out from the conversation. His mother was torn between expressing her relief that Luke wasn't too badly hurt, and sympathising with her husband. His father was looking grey with weariness, or was that shock?

He was right. He couldn't manage the farm on his own. Robbie came to a decision.

'I'll help you,' he said. The words were out before he had chance to consider. But really, did he have any other option? He had to make reparations somehow.

'What?' His father looked quite put out to be stopped in mid-tirade.

His mother said, 'But Robbie, your own job . . . '

'I'd already booked two weeks' holiday to be home whilst Luke was on his honeymoon. I'll see if they'll let me start that a bit sooner, take some unpaid leave. And if they won't, well, I'll hand in my notice.' He kept his voice neutral, not letting them see how much it would hurt to turn his back on his work.

'But you love that job,' said his mother, her normally olive complexion pale from yet another shock. 'You can't do that.'

'About time he did something for the family,' said Robbie's father and sniffed. He didn't even say thank you.

★   ★   ★

After a couple of days of taking it easy, Mr Jackson seemed once again to be on the road to recovery.

To celebrate the improvement in his appetite, Hope decided to cook a special meal. She was beginning to work out his likes and dislikes and knew a 'nice bit of fish' went down well. She had found parsley growing in the garden and enjoyed herself preparing cod in a fresh parsley sauce.

'That smells good,' said Mr Jackson when she put his plate down in front of him. The last couple of days he had already been in bed by this time, but today he had chosen to eat in the kitchen with Hope.

'I hope you like it. The potatoes are from Mrs Simpson's garden and the peas are from the Ashburys'. It's amazing how many people here grow their own veg, and how kind they are at sharing it.'

Mr Jackson frowned at her, puzzled. 'It's aye been like that round here.'

For a while they ate in silence. Hope was beginning to get used to the old man and she no longer worried if he didn't want to chat.

When she brought out strawberries for dessert he smiled approvingly and said, 'Your grandad used to grow grand strawberries.'

Hope froze at this topic, but Mr Jackson seemed not to notice.

'He was a fine gardener, so he was.

Your gran, now, she would rather stay inside the house, but Joseph was happy to be out in all weathers. He'd learnt that from his own dad, of course. Joseph Senior had to grow food if he was going to keep a family of five growing boys fed.'

Hope was surprised out of her determination to show no interest. 'Were there really five children? At Cleughbrae? But the place is tiny.'

'Aye, so were most houses,' said Mr Jackson, looking at her as if she was mad. 'People managed. You'd have two or three bairns to a double bed often as not. Never did them any harm.'

'I suppose not,' said Hope doubtfully. She still thought it must have been very cramped, with seven people living in that little house. 'You said there were five boys?'

'Aye. The boys were a fair bit older than me, like. We weren't friendly but I knew of the family. The oldest boy, Tom, was killed in the First World War.'

Hope couldn't stop herself asking,

111

'What happened to the others?'

Mr Jackson frowned, narrowing his eyes as though trying to remember. 'The next two brothers, I cannae mind their names, they emigrated to Canada. Norman was the fourth one. He stayed at home, never married. Joseph was the youngest and we all thought he wouldn't marry, either, and then he and Jane Irving got together. I remember their engagement. My mother insisted on taking me along to congratulate them, I cannae mind why. I was about eighteen at the time and they seemed ever so old.' He smiled reminiscently. 'I couldn't imagine why they'd want to get married, at their age.'

'That was during the Second World War?'

'Aye, it would have been.'

'Did you go to their wedding?'

'No, I don't recall that I did. It was just a low key thing. Weddings often were then.'

'And after the wedding they went to

live at Cleughbrae? Weren't Joseph's parents living there then?'

'I'm not sure where they lived at first. You could ask Susie Ashbury about that. She knew the family better than I did.'

'Maybe I will,' said Hope, already knowing she wouldn't. It was one thing talking to Mr Jackson about her family. He hadn't known her then, it wasn't his fault she hadn't been told the truth. Susie was another thing entirely.

★   ★   ★

'I'm not sure telling Hope about her mother and the whole adoption thing went as well as I'd hoped,' said Susie.

She and Simon and Sarah were having a few moments peace over morning coffee whilst the two grandchildren ran round and round the garden like wild things.

Simon grunted, 'I told you not to interfere.'

'I think she needed to know the truth,' said Sarah. 'But maybe you could have broken it to her in a different way?'

'Such as?' Susie felt quite hurt. She had just been doing her best.

'I don't know. But it was obviously a huge shock to her, that's why she doesn't want to talk about it with any of us. Maybe if you could have prepared her better in advance? But it's too late for that now,' said Simon, matter-of-fact as ever.

Susie sighed. She had enjoyed seeing more of her goddaughter and was missing her.

Sarah said, 'Why don't we take the children to see her and Mr Jackson later on? We've got to keep in touch, even if she doesn't want to talk about you-know-what.'

'That's not be a bad idea,' said Susie, cheering up. Hope seemed quite fond of Megan and Josh and if the children were there it would help the conversation along.

'Make sure you don't push her,' said Simon.

'As if I would . . . '

★   ★   ★

Hope was making soup for Mr Jackson's lunch when she heard the knock at the door. Who was it now she wondered. Perhaps one of the old men from the village come to hide from his own wife and keep Mr Jackson company. That was the sort of visitor her patient enjoyed, someone who would play dominoes and reminisce about how much better things used to be — and wouldn't nag about whether he was eating properly or doing his exercises.

Hope dried her hands and went to answer the door. Mr Jackson could have gone himself but he had got in to the habit of leaving it to her. When she saw who it was, she was glad she had answered. Standing on the wide stone doorstep were not just Susie, and Sarah, and the two grandchildren, but

115

Maria Mackenzie as well. Mr Jackson would definitely have been overfaced.

'Any more?' she asked, only half joking, as they all trooped in.

Susie kissed her cheek. 'How are you dear? The children wanted to come round and see you and we popped in on Maria on the way and she felt she could do with a little outing and . . . '

'Lovely to see you all,' said Hope, trying to keep her doubts out of her voice. 'Why don't you come through to the kitchen and I'll see if Mr Jackson is up to having visitors just now?'

Mr Jackson expressed a willingness to see Megan and Josh, so Susie took them along to the front room where they would no doubt be given a choice from the 'secret' stash of toffees. Mr Jackson had a surprising soft spot for children. Hope thought it was a shame he wasn't able to see his own grandchildren. There had been talk of the family coming over for a visit from Australia, but nothing had been confirmed so far.

Hope and Sarah and Maria were left in the kitchen.

'How's Luke?' asked Hope. She still felt guilty at her relief it wasn't Robbie who had been injured.

'Making good progress. All being well, he's coming home tomorrow.' Maria Mackenzie was sitting at the kitchen table, tracing patterns in the wood with her finger, and not looking nearly as happy as Hope would have expected.

'That's good,' she said encouragingly.

'Things are a bit difficult at Holm Farm just now,' said Sarah, seeming to feel some explanation was needed. 'Robbie and his dad are not exactly seeing eye-to-eye, which is why Maria thought she'd come for a walk with us.'

'Oh dear.' Hope hardly knew Robbie's father, but she had always found the son remarkably good-natured.

'They're both hard workers, of course they are,' said Maria. 'But they have their own ideas about how things should be done. It was good of Robbie to take time off work to help. But now I'm wondering if it was the best thing . . . And once we have Luke back in the house it'll be even worse. Now John has got over his relief Luke's injury isn't anything worse, he's pretty annoyed about the whole thing.'

'I'm sure it'll be fine. Every family has their tiffs,' said Sarah. 'And you've got a lot on your hands at the moment, what with the wedding so near. It's not surprising people are getting a little short-tempered.'

'Ah, yes, the wedding,' said Maria, brightening at once and launching into a long and detailed exposition of all the things that still needed to be done and the problems that had arisen with the dresses. These problems didn't seem to get her down the way family arguments did.

Hope listened with one ear as she added more lentils and stock to the soup and dug an extra loaf out of the freezer. She would, of course, invite everyone to stay for lunch. It was a good thing lentil soup could be easily stretched.

Mr Jackson chose to eat his lunch on a tray in the sitting room. All the visitors except Maria were persuaded to stay and join Hope in the kitchen.

'Wonderful soup,' said Susie, smiling at Hope fondly. Hope felt guilty for having avoided her godmother. 'I'd forgotten what a good cook you are. You take after your mother.'

Hope frowned. She didn't want to be reminded of her mother. Sarah seemed to realise this and jumped in to change the direction of the conversation.

'The Mackenzies have got just about everything sorted for Luke's wedding,' she said. 'Even the flower fiasco seems to be in hand. It's just the bridesmaids' dresses Maria's still worried about. You know Claire's sister is expecting, and the dress-maker was going to make last minute alterations depending on how much weight she had put on. Now the dressmaker has had to go away and they're not sure who they can get to do it.'

'Poor things,' said Susie sympathetically. 'If it's not one thing it's another. I remember the difficulties we had with the cake for your wedding. Do you remember someone dropped the top tier and it had to be completely redone?'

Sarah grinned. 'Of course I remember. You were in a complete panic.'

'I was not. Now, I wonder if there's anyone we know who could help Maria?'

This was Hope's chance to speak. She had been mulling it over since Maria's visit. She still felt hurt by the attitude of the village to her and her family's secrets. The fact that so many people had watched her and said nothing. But she felt she should offer. 'I've done a fair bit of dress-making in my time. I suppose, if they thought I was good enough, I could see if I could help out with the dresses . . . '

Susie clapped her hands. 'Of course. Why didn't I think of that?'

'I'm sure they'd really appreciate it,'

said Sarah. 'You're so clever with your fingers. Have you had the chance to do much sewing recently?'

'Actually, I have done a little.' Hope thought of the almost finished dress she had upstairs in her room, the one destined for Megan. She had stopped working on it when Susie dropped her bombshell. 'Actually, I started making a dress for Megan. She might not like it, but I felt like doing something with my hands. If you want, we can go up and have a look at it after lunch.'

'A dress for me?' said the little girl, blue eyes wide with excitement. 'A proper dress made just for me?'

'Yes. It's nothing too fancy, and if you don't like it you must just say, it's not a problem.'

'That's really kind of you,' said Susie, putting a hand on Hope's arm. She looked relieved. She probably thought this meant Hope had forgiven her. And, to some extent, Hope supposed it did. After all, it wasn't Susie's fault her mother had kept that secret.

Robbie Clashes With His Father

There were many tasks around the farm Robbie loved doing. Cutting and baling the hay, for example, was something he'd willingly volunteer for. Milking, on the other hand, he had never enjoyed, and now he had to do it once if not twice a day for weeks to come. He was seriously regretting his offer to help out.

In the last few years, Luke had taken over responsibility for most of the milking chores. This meant, unfortunately, they now fell to Robbie. His father helped out in the morning, being naturally an early riser, but the afternoon milking was Robbie's job entirely. This made it marginally better, as there was less chance of arguments. But really, standing for what seemed like hours in the milking parlours bored him to tears. He preferred to be out in the hills, checking on the plants and the water courses and breathing in the clean air.

The air in here was anything but sweetly scented, and more than once he had stood at the back of a cow at the wrong time. Awful! It was the only thing that had made his father smile for days.

He was thinking these gloomy thoughts during the afternoon milking when he heard the sliding doors open and his mother appeared, followed by Hope McIlroy. She was the very last person he expected to see here.

'Hope has never seen cows being milked, so I thought I'd bring her along,' said his mother happily. 'It's funny, isn't it, that what is run of the mill for us is completely new for other people?'

He was glad to see that she had cheered up. His latest row with his father, over the best use of the field by the river, had really upset her that morning. 'I'll leave Hope here with you, she can find her own way back when she's seen enough.'

Robbie smiled his understanding. His mother wasn't too fond of the milking parlour herself. He took Hope's arm and brought her to stand beside him.

'It's amazing,' said Hope, gazing around. She seemed genuinely interested. Robbie looked around the cavernous building, trying to see it through her eyes. There were the cows lined up on each side, one to a cubicle. They munched contentedly on their cake, each attached to an automatic milking unit. He found himself explaining how these worked, how the milk was carried from these directly to the bulk storage tank.

Hope smiled at him. 'It's much more high tech than I expected.'

'That's Luke's doing. My father is a bit set in his ways, but when Luke took over the dairy side he updated all the equipment, even introduced a computer to calculate the amount of feed needed.' At times Robbie wished his brother hadn't been so keen on computerising everything. It meant he not only had to re-acquaint himself with the animals, but also had to learn how to use the blasted computer system.

'We never really think about where milk comes from, do we?' said Hope, still peering around.

It seemed so strange to have her here, in her pretty skirt and sandals, amongst the animals and the strong farm smells. He was impressed that she didn't seem at all troubled by them. He'd had one or two girlfriends who had run a mile if a cow so much as twitched its ears.

'How're you doing?' he said. He had seen nothing of her for days. The farm seemed to have taken over his life.

'I'm fine,' she said quickly.

'Mr Jackson keeping all right?'

'Not too bad. He is getting better, but it's a slow process.'

'And I bet he doesn't always do what he's told?'

Hope gave a brief smile. 'Not always.'

Robbie could feel his whole day improving, just from having her stand beside him and give that shy smile. He could do this. And it wouldn't be forever, Luke would want to be back to work as soon as he possibly could.

'Luke's coming home tomorrow,' he said, thinking of this.

'Yes, your mother said. I came up to offer to help with the bridesmaids' dresses.'

'You did?' said Robbie, confused.

'Yes. I'm not a professional dress-maker, of course, but she's showed me the alterations that need doing and I think I can manage them.'

'That's very kind of you.' Robbie had a hazy recollection of his mother and Claire in consternated discussion about the dresses. There had been so many 'crises' he tended to switch off when they were mentioned.

'I'll enjoy it,' said Hope simply. 'And

it's something I can do when I'm in the house with Mr Jackson. Which reminds me, I'd better get back. I just popped out whilst he was having his afternoon rest.'

Robbie gave a quick glance around the cows, who all seemed fine, and decided he could leave them for a moment and walk back to the house with her. An idea had occurred to him.

As soon as they were out in the relatively fresh air of the farmyard he said, 'I wonder if you'd like to come to the wedding yourself? I mean, as my partner.'

Hope let the long hair fall over her face for a moment, and when she pushed it back he saw she was blushing. 'Your mum has already invited me, actually. She said it was the least she could do.'

'Oh,' said Robbie, feeling foolish now. 'Well, that's good, if you're going to be there. You'll maybe save a dance for me?'

'I'm not sure that I can go. It's not

easy for Mr Jackson to do even simple things like getting himself on and off the bed. I don't like to leave him alone too long.'

'But he's getting better all the time.' Robbie now felt it was essential she be there. 'The wedding isn't for another ten days, who knows how mobile he'll be by then?'

'I said to your mother I would think about it. I don't want to cause her a problem with seating arrangements so I should probably just say no . . . '

'Forget the seating arrangements!' said Robbie, allowing his exasperation with the whole ridiculous palaver to show. 'They're not set in stone. Honestly, we can work something out, and it would be great if you could come.'

'Thanks,' she said, seeming surprised at his enthusiasm. He was rather surprised himself.

'In fact, I've got an idea about Mr Jackson . . . ' But what the idea was he didn't have the chance to explain just then. The cows were starting to get restless and he could hear them mooing and stamping the ground. The last thing he needed was for one of them to kick off the milk unit. 'I'll call round and explain later,' he said, and slipped back through the door into the gloom.

* * *

Hope found she was humming to herself as she made her way back to Kirkside. She went by way of the road, not trusting herself to climb safely over the fences on the river path. It was a beautiful walk whichever way you went and for the first time in a while she felt she had something to be happy about.

She was now part of this little community. Everyone seemed to think she was doing a good job with Mr Jackson. Maria had been effusive in her thanks for the offer of help with the dresses. And best of all, Robbie had invited her to the wedding. OK, Maria had invited her too, which had been very kind, but it was Robbie's invitation that had made her heart soar.

And then, when she arrived back at Kirkside, she found a message asking her to phone Tommy Grainger and her mood plummeted. She wondered what he wanted now. Hadn't everything been sorted out since she had paid the money?

'The police have been in touch with me,' said the accountant, after they had exchanged pleasantries.

Hope was puzzled. 'The police? Why?' Had something else gone wrong?

'As you know, we've been trying to trace Miss Amy Jones in connection with certain assets that have gone missing from the business.'

'Ah. Yes.' Hope had forgotten the police had been involved in that. 'So . . . have they found her?'

'Indeed they have. She's moved to London and seems to be living there with her boyfriend. Steven Parker? She has been using his name, which is why it hasn't been easy to trace her.'

Hope had only known Amy's boy-friend by his first name, and had never liked him. She was almost certain things had started to go wrong with Amy when she came under the influence of this man.

'I thought you would like to know,' said Tommy, when Hope said nothing.

'Yes. Thanks. I suppose that's, er, good.'

'It helps move things forward. I can now pursue her for any assets she has relating to the business.'

'I suppose so,' said Hope. She hated all this. 'I thought that was all finished with.'

'Strictly speaking it is, as you have made sure that no one but yourself is out of pocket.' He still sounded disapproving. 'So what you need to consider is, do you want to try and pursue her for the losses she has caused you?'

'Me?' Hope didn't like to think of taking her best friend — former best friend — to court. Her immediate reaction was to say No! Of course, she had been furious with Amy when the truth had first come out. But now she felt at least some of the blame had been hers. She shouldn't have put so much temptation in her friend's way.

'You don't need to decide now,' said Tommy. 'Think it over. You have a solicitor of your own, don't you? Discuss it with him.'

'OK, I will,' said Hope, relieved not to have to make a decision right away.

When the conversation ended Hope's thoughts were in disarray. Amy had run away to start a new life in London and left Hope alone to deal with the collapse of the business. She shivered as she remembered confrontations with angry creditors, the horror of explaining what had happened to regular customers, the pain of seeing the shop denuded.

She had been so preoccupied with other things since arriving at St. Ann's Bridge she had hardly thought of all this. Especially since the revelations about her mother. Perhaps she should be grateful to Susie for that, at least.

★ ★ ★

On the Saturday after Luke's return, Robbie escaped from the lovey-dovey atmosphere of his brother and fiancée in the house. He went to check on one of the cows who was poorly — which was all Robbie's fault, according to his father. And it was just his bad luck to find his father as he took a detour through the lower field. Probably checking up on him.

'I see you're putting yourself out to help, as usual,' he said, his ruddy face grim.

'I've just checked on the poorly cow, and re-hung the bottom gate that hasn't worked properly for years,' said Robbie. 'I call that pretty useful.'

'The gate was fine,' said his father. 'It just needed a bit of extra muscle.'

Robbie shrugged. He knew the gate had been annoying Luke for months and he was pleased to have fixed it. He noticed his father couldn't even bring himself to mention the cow. He was furious about anything that kept milk yields down.

'Your mother was looking for you,' said his father. 'I don't think you boys realise what a lot of work you create for her, having you both at home and her never knowing whether you're coming or going.'

'Luke won't be living at home much longer,' said Robbie, wishing his father would move so he could start walking back to the house.

'And then there's the wedding. Your mother is driving herself distracted, but I don't see you lifting a finger to help out.'

This was really a bit much, coming from the father of the groom who, as far as Robbie could tell, had so far done absolutely nothing.

'At least I arranged the stag weekend,' he said.

'Aye, and we all know what a success

that was. Why on earth did you have to go off to the back of beyond?'

Robbie was about to repeat, because that was what Luke wanted, but managed to hold his tongue. That weekend was still an all-too-bitter memory. Luke breaking his leg had been bad, but it could have been so much worse.

'And I've arranged the band for the reception,' he said, pleased to think of something else. He was rather proud of this. The band, Abhainn, were one of the most popular ceilidh bands in the area. They had initially turned down the request to perform from Claire's mother, saying they already had two gigs that weekend and didn't fancy a third. But Robbie knew the band leader from school, and he'd talked them into it. He'd explained what a real community event this was going to be and how having the best band there would really top things off. The members of Abhainn, like most people, were susceptible to flattery.

They'd agreed to come along and Sam, the leader, had even suggested Robbie bring his own fiddle and join them in a couple of songs. That was flattery of an entirely different kind. Robbie hadn't played in public in ages. He was tempted, all the same.

'Let's hope nothing goes wrong with that, then,' said his father sourly, bringing Robbie back to the present with a bang. 'The way this wedding is going I'll be surprised if it doesn't.'

'Don't you want it all to go well?'

His dad pretended to be hurt then. 'Of course I do. That's why I'm worrying about all the difficulties. Someone's got to sort them out, and it's not likely to be you, is it?'

This time Robbie didn't wait for his father to move. He strode round him and headed off up the slope, not caring whether he was followed or not. No matter what he did, his father would always find the negative side.

The Wedding Day Arrives

On the day of Luke and Claire's marriage, Hope awoke to a beautiful early autumn morning. She drew her curtains and leant on the windowsill. The sun shone brightly on the dew-laden garden, with pools of white mist drifting in the hollows. Towards the river, the mist was thicker, but with sun this bright it was likely to clear later. A perfect day for a wedding.

And Hope was going to be there. Robbie had come up with the ideal solution to Mr Jackson: they would simply arrange for the old man to come along too. Of course, he had always been invited, but everyone assumed he wasn't well enough to attend. Robbie had popped around a couple of days after he had invited Hope to be his guest, to explain his idea. He had wanted to know whether

Mr Jackson would actually like to be there.

The answer had been yes. If Robbie could arrange transport, he would love to go. He hadn't said so, of course. He had said, 'Aye, I wouldnae mind a wee jaunt like.' But Hope knew him well enough now to interpret this.

Mr Jackson would attend both the ceremony in the kirk and the reception in the village hall. He could stay as long as he wanted. When he had had enough, Robbie had promised to take him home. 'And the lass can stay on,' Mr Jackson said firmly. 'I don't want her evening spoilt because of me.'

Mr Jackson's best suit, not worn for years, had been sent to the cleaners, and Hope had decided to make a brand new dress for herself.

She decided to use a piece of pale turquoise silk and was tempted into trying a completely new style. This material didn't lend itself to a long floaty skirt. It needed to be fitted, and so she had created a long sheath of a dress, high-necked and short sleeved, with a split up the back to allow her to walk. With a little cream jacket she already owned and a new hat she had found in a department store in Dumfries, she felt she was going to look very smart indeed. She just hoped she hadn't overdone it.

Things were frantic in the Mackenzie household. Robbie and his father tried to hurry through all the normal chores so as to be free by lunchtime. The afternoon milking had been entrusted, much against his father's judgement, to a friend of a friend from near Lockerbie. The problem with a big wedding like this was that everyone they knew was going to be there. Robbie just hoped this man turned out to be reliable. If not, he knew who would be to blame.

Once the farm business was out of the way there was the question of getting kitted out in their finery and off to the church on time. Luke was still using crutches and needed help to get dressed. This task fell, of course, to Robbie.

'Lucky you're wearing a kilt and not a dress suit or you'd never be able to get into it,' he said as he untangled his brother's sporran.

Once they arrived at the church things improved. With Robbie's help Luke managed to limp to the front pew. Robbie checked he had the rings, and then felt he could finally relax. If anything went wrong now, it couldn't be his fault.

The ceremony was beautiful. He hadn't expected it to be. The rehearsal had been rushed and bad-tempered, like much of the past couple of weeks. But once the Wedding March started and they turned to see Claire advancing towards them, all those worries fell away.

She was a pretty enough girl, but today she looked radiant. Robbie watched his brother's smile grow wider and wider as she approached and wondered what it would feel like to be

Luke. To be so sure you wanted to stay with one person for ever, to be so happy to see them walking slowly towards you.

The whole thing seemed to take a matter of minutes. Neither bride nor groom fluffed their lines and Robbie was on hand to prop up his brother when he turned a little too quickly and almost fell. The walk back down the aisle, with Luke using crutches, wasn't quite as picturesque as it might have been, but nobody seemed to mind.

Hope was enjoying herself more than she had in months. She had decided not to rush into any decision about what action, if any, she should take regarding Amy. She had puzzled over it on and off for days and come to no conclusion.

Another weekend wouldn't make any difference. And she felt happy here among these people. She was sure it was nothing to do with family connection to the village or all the nonsense that Susie Ashbury might want to think, it was simply that everyone was so friendly and welcoming.

The wedding ceremony was lovely. Even Mr Jackson said it brought a tear to his eye. And afterwards he sat in his wheelchair for a while so Hope didn't have to worry about him whilst the photographs were taken. There seemed to be hundreds of them. First of all in the doorway of the little red sandstone church, with the strange narrow bell-tower overhead. And then by the arched gateway. And then down by the river. The bride looked gorgeous, of course, but Hope was quietly proud of the bridesmaids' appearances, too. The little adjustments she had made to their dresses meant they fitted perfectly.

Hope and Mr Jackson remained near the church whilst the rest of the party made their way across the uneven ground towards the water. For a moment there was quiet. Hope glanced at the graveyard behind her and thought again of that stone she had found, Jane and Joseph's grave.

'Aye, they're all there,' said Mr Jackson.

'Mmm,' said Hope. What did he mean, all? What other relatives did she have buried here? She shivered. She didn't want to think of that now. Today was a day for optimism and thoughts of the future.

She was glad when they left the grave-yard and moved on to the reception in the village hall. At first she thought it was strange to have the reception here. It wasn't very smart, and from what she had seen of the Mackenzies and Claire's family they could have afforded something grander. But now it seemed just right. It had been decorated with flowers from the local gardens and the walls hung with tartan banners. The tables were all covered in snowy-white linen. It was big enough to fit in everyone they had invited.

Robbie helped her manoeuvre Mr Jackson's chair up the steps and into the hall.

'I can walk fine if you give me my stick,' said the old man grumpily.

'Whatever you prefer,' said Hope. 'We can leave your chair by the entrance and you can sit on the same seats as everyone else.'

'Although the seats aren't all that comfortable, with the bits of ivy Claire and her sister have been winding around them,' said Robbie.

'We had left a space for your chair over there by Mr Wellburn,' continued Hope. 'I thought it was an ideal position, near the wall and you'd be a bit higher so you'd be able to see everything.'

'All right then,' said Mr Jackson. 'You put me where you want and go and get yourselves settled.' He still sounded grouchy, but if he had really objected he would have insisted on having his own way.

'I wish you were sitting up at the top table with me,' said Robbie softly as he and Hope searched the tables for her own place. 'You look so beautiful. I don't want to let you out of my sight.'

Hope felt herself blush. 'You don't look so bad yourself. I don't think I've ever seen so many men in kilts.'

It was true, Robbie looked stunning in his green, black and red tartan, with the pristine white shirt and black dress jacket. Most of the other men looked good, too, but nothing compared to him. Maybe it was his thick dark curls, or the way his eyes laughed when they met hers — or maybe she was just biased?

'I always liked an excuse to dress up,' he said lightly. 'My mum's waving me over, I'd better go. I'll catch up with you later?'

Hope had been seated at a table with the Ashburys. Sarah's husband had come down for the wedding and her brother, Steven, and his wife were there, too. Hope and Susie had almost regained their old affectionate relationship and she enjoyed chatting to the family.

'How're you finding living in St.

Ann's Bridge?' asked Steven. He was a younger, slimmer version of his father and had also trained as a doctor, although he had gone into hospital medicine. 'It's not a bad little place.'

'It's lovely. Everyone is so friendly.'

'Yes. Not at all like living in a big city.' Steven grinned. He and his wife lived and worked in Manchester so he would know all about big cities.

'I always hoped you'd move back here one day,' said Susie, eyeing her son fondly.

'Yes, I know, and take over Dad's GP practice. No thanks, Mum. That was never going to happen.'

'Nothing wrong with being a GP,' said his father.

'I know, I know. It's just not what I wanted to do. Anyway, we were talking about Hope, not me. How long are you here for? Any plans for the future?'

'Er . . . no,' said Hope. She knew she should have plans, but somehow hadn't been able to make any. 'I'll stay with Mr Jackson as long as he wants me, which I think will be another month at least.'

'And you can come back to stay with us after that,' said Susie.

'And you promised to visit us in Edinburgh,' said Sarah. 'You know that you are Megan's all-time favourite person after making that dress for her.'

'I'd like that,' said Hope. She had never been to Edinburgh before. But none of these suggestions were proper plans for the future.

'I think you should wait until everything is sorted out with *Material Things* before you make any big decisions,' said Susie. Hope should have been grateful for her support, but she suspected it was mostly because Susie wanted her to stay in St. Ann's Bridge for as long as possible. Susie liked having her around, which was flattering, but at some point Hope would need to get back to her own life.

'*Material Things?*' asked Sarah's husband, puzzled by the name.

'The shop Hope used to own,' said

Sarah, giving him a meaningful look.

'Let's not talk about that now,' said Hope. She was feeling guilty because she hadn't told Susie that Amy had been traced. She hadn't told anyone about that. It was easier that way.

'You know, if you had the time, I'd appreciate it if you would make an evening dress for me,' said Sarah out of the blue. 'I'd pay you, of course. Every year Paul's company have a big St. Andrew's Day ball and I never know what to wear. If you could make me something I'd be very grateful.'

'What a good idea,' said Susie, a little too quickly, so Hope suspected this was something the two of them had concocted together.

'I don't know . . . ' she said.

'Think about it at least.'

Hope felt she couldn't refuse to do that. She wouldn't mind doing more sewing, and a ball gown would be fun. She just didn't like to feel she was being pushed into things. With Susie around, it was hard not to be.

★　★　★

Robbie was starting to feel nervous. It was nearly time for his speech. He didn't know why he'd agreed to do this. Standing up with Luke in the church was one thing, but he had never liked public speaking. This was going to be an ordeal, not helped by having his father glowering at him along the table.

He felt a hand on his shoulder and turned to see his mother behind him. 'You'll be brilliant,' she said. 'It's been a perfect day. I'm so proud of both my boys.'

She topped up his glass and returned to her seat in time for the Master of Ceremonies, Simon Ashbury, to call everybody to order. Robbie took a long drink. Either that or his mother's words gave him the boost he needed. By the time Simon called him he knew exactly what he was going to say.

It wasn't a brilliant speech, but it wasn't bad. Everyone laughed at all the right places and he managed the toast to the bridesmaids without making a mess of it. Luke glared at him when he mentioned one or two youthful indiscretions, which was just as it should be. He made a teasing reference to his mother's managing ways and received a thumbs up from Luke and a grin from her. She could take a joke, that was one of her many good qualities. When it was over he sat down with a great sigh of relief. Now he could start to enjoy himself.

He looked around for Hope McIlroy. She was sitting with the Ashbury family and seemed to be having a good time. She had applauded him enthusiastically. As soon as the last speech was over he was going to head down there to join her.

Unfortunately, as Dr Ashbury rounded everything off, Robbie was accosted by the fiddler from the ceilidh band, Abhainn.

'Can I have a word?' he said, hustling Robbie to one side. 'We've got a bit of a problem.'

'What kind of problem?' Robbie was already worried. The man's face was tense. Looking around, Robbie couldn't see any of the other band members.

'Sam's no' well,' said the man, Johnny.

Sam was the band leader, who called the dances and occasionally sang.

'What's wrong? Is it serious?'

'He thinks it's food poisoning. There's no way he can go on stage.'

'So . . . ?' Robbie's mind was racing. Was this going to mean they had no band after all? It would be a disaster, ceilidh dancing was something they'd all been looking forward to. 'What's going to happen? Do you have anyone who can step in?'

'No one we know is free.' Johnny eyed Robbie with interest. 'But Sam says perhaps you can do it? Did you no' play in a band together a while ago?'

'That was years ago! And I can't call the dances, or sing. I play the fiddle and I don't even do that well.' Robbie was horrified.

'I play the fiddle myself, but I can call the dances if I have to. I just can't do that and play at the same time. Sam was suggesting you do most of the playing and I'll do his stuff. You've brought your fiddle along, like?'

'Yes, but . . . ' Robbie would have been happy enough to play along to a song or two, in the background. What Johnny was suggesting was entirely different. 'Look, I haven't practiced much. I won't know half the songs.'

'As it happens, I've got the music with me. And when I'm not calling I'll play with you. Sam thinks you'll do fine.'

'Sam hasn't heard me play for years!'

Johnny regarded him calmly. Now he had explained the dilemma, he seemed to feel he had transferred all his worries to Robbie. 'Do you have any other suggestions?'

'Well . . . no.'

'Fine, then. Bill, the drummer, has run Sam home. You'd better go and tell them we'll start a wee bit late, say in fifteen minutes. Get your fiddle and we'll have a few practice runs out the back here.'

Robbie couldn't see any other option. He went to explain the situation to Claire and Luke, ignoring his parents' worried looks. As he hurried off to find his violin he felt physically sick. He didn't even have chance to say a word to Hope. This was turning into a nightmare.

★   ★   ★

Hope wondered what was going on. There appeared to be some problem. Robbie had disappeared, hurried back in for a quick consultation with Luke and Claire then disappeared again. She had been looking forward to spending some time with him and had been almost sure he would join her soon. Now it didn't seem that was going to happen.

She decided to keep herself busy by checking on Mr Jackson.

She made her way between the tables and found herself being stopped more than once to share appreciation of the ceremony in the church, the speeches, how lovely Claire was looking, and even comments on her own dress. She was beginning to wish she had made something a little less noticeable.

Eventually she reached the table where Mr Jackson was sitting. Maria had placed him with other elderly people from the village, most of whom Hope already knew from their visits to the house. At first they had intimidated her with their strong accents and dour demeanour, but as she grew to know them she realised she rather liked them.

'How are you all doing?' she asked cheerfully, sliding in to the seat beside Mr Jackson which was temporarily vacant.

'No so bad,' he said, nodding his high-domed head in quite a merry way.

'He's had a wee drop of the whisky and it's cheered him no end,' said one of the men who sometimes came to play dominoes.

'Not too much,' said Hope quickly. 'You know what the doctor said.'

'Killjoys, the lot of them,' said Mr Jackson, but for once he didn't sound too annoyed. Hope was glad he had agreed to come along. Just so long as he didn't overdo things.

Whilst she was trying to think of a way to say this, tactfully, the elderly lady whose seat she had taken reappeared. She moved slowly with the aid of a stick. Hope knew her by sight and as she vacated the chair Mr Jackson introduced her as, 'Mrs. Slater. She's lived in St. Ann's Bridge as long as I can remember.'

The name sounded familiar, but Hope had heard so many new names in the last few months that she couldn't immediately place it.

'Nice to meet you at last,' said the woman, looking Hope up and down from rheumy eyes. 'A fine young woman you've turned out to be. I mind your mother when she was wee. You're nothing like her.'

Hope was rather thrown by the comment. After a moment, when no one spoke, she said, 'I suppose I take after my father.'

'There's maybe a wee bit of Johnny McIlroy in you,' said the old lady, her head on one side. 'Not that I knew him so well. His family only moved here when he was in his teens and his parents passed away young. Not been so lucky with family, have you?'.

Hope murmured something unspecific, not quite sure how she was supposed to answer that.

'You know who you remind me of most? Elspeth's mother, when she was young. She was the prettiest thing you ever saw, with her long curls, just like yours. I suppose that was why her dad kept her in the house so much. He knew there'd be trouble if he let her out.'

Hope was aware of everyone around the table watching her, waiting to hear more. Mrs Slater, with her sparse white hair and deeply wrinkled face, was probably the oldest of them. She would remember Jane Calvert the best. What did she mean, about Jane's father keeping her in the house? It sounded sinister.

'I — I don't think I've seen a picture of my grandmother when she was young.' Hope had hardly seen any pictures of her grandparents at all.

'She was a pretty wee thing,' said Mrs Slater. 'Poor lassie. There are things I could tell you about her and her family.' For some reason she looked at Mr Jackson with narrowed eyes, thoughtful.

Hope wanted her to stop talking right then. She didn't want to hear any more about her family. She didn't want all these people staring at her, fascinated.

Perhaps Mr Jackson realised this. He said, 'Hope's no' so much interested in family matters. If you don't mind, I think I'll be heading home now. Do you think you can find someone to give me a hand?'

'I'll take you home,' said Hope, a great wave of relief flooding over her. 'I'll get one of Luke's friends to help us get the chair down the steps and the rest I can manage myself. I should have suggested it sooner, I hope you aren't too tired?'

She hurried off to find their coats and ask someone to assist with the chair, pleased to have something to occupy her.

She had almost forgotten Robbie in her eagerness to escape Mrs Slater. The last thing she expected, therefore, was to see him and another young man standing together in the car park at the side of the hall. They were playing violins! What on earth was going on?

Mr Jackson nodded at them, looking interested. 'Now, I didn't know Robbie Mackenzie was back playing in a band. I wonder what his dad has to say about that.'

'Does Robbie play in a band?' Hope thought there was no end to the surprises this evening.

'He used to. My wife quite liked listening to them. The ceilidh music, you know.'

Mr Jackson looked like he wanted to stay and listen himself, but Hope just needed to get home. She turned the chair on to the pavement and began to chat brightly about how lovely the wedding had been.

* * *

Robbie saw Hope leaving, but he didn't have time to speak to her. He didn't have time for anything! How could he get up to speed with more than a dozen ceilidh songs he hadn't played in public for years and learn at least a dozen new ones, all in less than half an hour?

'You're no' doing badly,' said Johnny with apparent approval. 'You must've been keeping the practice up? Your finger work's fine.'

'Thanks.' Robbie could feel the sweat trickling down his back at the thought of exposing his inadequacy in public.

His right arm was already aching with the constant use of the bow.

'I think we'll start with *Megan's Wedding* and the other two reels. You know those and it'll get you into the swing of it. Then we'll do *Kate Dalrymple* and see how we get on from there. Aye, that's what we'll do.'

'OK,' said Robbie, resigned. He wasn't sure he could remember anything he had been told in the last fifteen minutes. He'd just have to hope it came back to him once he was on stage. He wished the fiddle wasn't always the instrument that had to carry the tune. He wished he had never learnt to play the thing.

'Here's Bill. We'll explain to him what we're doing and then get back inside.'

Robbie knew he had to do this. It was Luke's wedding and he couldn't let anything spoil it. And he had to prove to his father he wasn't completely useless. The music had been delayed long enough already. He took deep breaths and tried to look calm as he followed the other two band members back in to the hall.

* * *

'You'll be going back up to the hall now I'm settled?' said Mr Jackson. He looked rather pale and tired, lying back against the white pillows. Hope was worried she had let him do too much.

'I don't think so. I'll take Lucy for a short walk then I'll call it a night. I'm quite tired myself.'

'Rubbish. A young thing like you can't be tired. You'll soon brighten up once you start dancing.'

'I won't know any of the dances. I've never been to a ceilidh before.' This hadn't worried Hope when she thought Robbie would be around to show her what to do. Now she didn't think she could be bothered.

Mr Jackson ignored her protest. 'You'll be fine. The lads will be falling over themselves to show you the steps.

And don't you want to go and hear Robbie Mackenzie play his fiddle? You've got to go back and tell me how he does.'

Hope wasn't sure if Mr Jackson was interested in hearing about success or failure, but she realised she would like to hear Robbie herself. The fresh air and silence had helped her recover from the discomfort caused by old Mrs Slater. She was just being silly, to run away like that.

''OK, I'll go back for a while. But I'll leave the phone beside you here, and I'll keep checking my mobile. Call me at once if you need me.'

'I'm going to sleep,' said Mr Jackson firmly, removing his hearing aid. 'Put the light out. You can pop Lucy in here before you go.' His voice softened, as always, when he spoke of his dog. Hope took the old girl for a wander around the garden and then slipped her back into her master's bedroom.

She walked slowly back up the hill to the village hall. There were no street lights out here but the faint moonlight was enough to see by. She didn't feel at all nervous walking alone in the near-darkness. There was something about St. Ann's Bridge that felt safe. Not always happy, but safe.

She could hear the music long before she reached the hall. Lively tunes she didn't recognise, lilting across the quiet night. She quickened her step. It sounded like they were having fun in there.

The hall was a different place from the one Hope had left an hour or so earlier. The lights had been dimmed and tables moved back to clear a large space for dancing. And a large space was needed! More than half the guests seemed to be on their feet, ranging from toddlers to sprightly pensioners. Hope slipped into a seat where she guessed the Ashburys had been sitting — all of them were currently on the floor — and settled down to watch.

The dancing was great fun. It reminded Hope of barn dances she had been to at college. There was a definite structure to the dances and most people seemed to have some idea of what they were supposed to be doing. If they made mistakes, it didn't seem to matter. These were treated with good natured howls of laughter.

Hope enjoyed watching. A man on the stage announced the dance and gave instructions on the number of people in a set. Then he made them walk through the dance without music. Then they went through it again with the music, the man still calling out instructions. After that people were left to do their best, until the next dance began.

On the stage were three men; the tall thin one calling the dances, one at the back on drums, and Robbie Mackenzie with his violin. He was amazing. He seemed totally engrossed in the music, communing with his instrument, and playing the most amazing jigs and reels that had Hope tapping her feet. She noticed Maria watching her son with pride and relief on her face, and applauding loudly at each change of dance. Hope applauded too. She wondered why Robbie's father wasn't looking more pleased.

When the caller announced the next dance would be a *Dashing White Sergeant* Sarah appeared at Hope's side.

'Come on, we need you.' She took her hand and pulled her to her feet.

'But I don't know how to do it.'

'Never mind, it's easy. And you have to dance in threes so come and join Steven and me.'

Hope allowed herself to be towed along. She really wasn't sure she could do this. She didn't even understand half the words the man on the stage called out. What did it mean, *set to your partner*?

'Just copy what we do,' said Sarah. 'And don't worry if you make a mistake, so does everyone else!'

'You'll be fine,' said Steven cheerfully.

And Hope discovered, after a tentative start, that she was. The pattern of the dance was repeated over and over again, so once she got the hang of it she didn't have to work so hard at remembering. She could just enjoy the clapping of hands and stamping of feet, the twirling of the other dancers as they linked arms, and the fun of running through the archway of hands and joining up with another threesome.

After that, the only time Hope stopped dancing was when she went to check her mobile in case Mr Jackson had called, or when she needed a drink. She was having such fun. It was a shame Robbie was up on the stage and not down here dancing with her, but even that had its positive side. It was wonderful to see him playing, relaxing into the rhythm, his kilt swinging as he tapped his foot. Previously Hope had thought he looked very un-Scottish, with his dark colouring, but this evening he seemed the embodiment of the country, with his tartan and his music.

'Right, we're taking a break,' said the thin man who had been giving instructions. 'I believe the cake is going to be cut, then the bride and groom will take their leave. After that, if anyone wants to dance a wee bit more, we'll be back on stage.'

Hope made her way to where the Ashburys were sitting. She watched Robbie exchange a couple of jokes with the other band members and then jump down from the stage. She thought he would go back to his family, but he didn't. This time he came over to her.

'You were brilliant,' Hope said, as she pulled out a chair for him. 'I didn't realise you could play the violin, at least I did, but not like that.' She felt this evening had revealed a whole new side to him.

Robbie held out one hand towards her and she saw it was trembling. 'I didn't know I could play like that, either,' he said with a shake of his head.

'And I'm not sure I can do it again, if they want us to play another set. Phew! That was hard work.'

'But amazing. I loved it,' said Hope. She wanted to keep him to herself, but already the Ashburys were leaning in, offering their own congratulations.

'Excellent music,' said Simon.

'What happened to the usual fiddler?' asked Susie. 'You don't normally play with them, do you?'

Robbie began to explain how one member had fallen ill and he had been drafted in as a last minute replacement.

They all fell quiet whilst the cake was cut and pictures taken of Luke and Claire, still looking blissfully happy. Then the couple slipped away to change, and Robbie pushed the thick hair back from his forehead and said, 'It's hot in here. I think I'll take the chance to go outside and cool down.' He hesitated and then said more softly to Hope, 'Do you want to come and keep me company?'

Wishing she didn't blush so easily,

Hope nodded. 'That would be nice. I'm pretty hot myself, from all the dancing.'

She saw Susie smile approvingly as they stood up to leave. She wondered what on earth her godmother was thinking. They were far too old and sensible to be slipping outside for an illicit kiss. They were just good friends, and it was kind of Robbie to invite her.

It was completely dark outside, once you moved out of the circle of the hall lights. The soft breeze brought with it the scent of autumn, leaves newly fallen, a heavy dew. Hope looked up at the sky and saw so many stars it was as though someone had scattered sand up there.

'The Milky Way,' said Robbie, seeing where she looked. 'It's not often so clear.'

'I didn't see the stars much, when I lived down south.'

'You don't when you live in the city. Too much man-made light. That's why I love it out here.'

'A lot of people would feel nervous,

with so much darkness.'

'Do you?'

'No.'

They were silent for a while. Robbie had taken her hand to lead her to a bench at the back of the hall, facing out across the fields.

'What will you do when Mr Jackson is fully recovered?' he asked. 'Go back down south?'

'I don't know,' said Hope, shifting uneasily. 'I wish everyone wouldn't keep asking me that.'

'Sorry. It's just . . . ' He paused and she felt him turn towards her. 'I'd like to ask you out, for a drink or a meal. But I don't know if you're going away soon. Or if there is someone waiting for you back there.'

Hope could feel her heart begin to thud. 'There's no one waiting for me.'

'So we could go out sometime, if you're not disappearing just yet?'

'I'd like that.'

'Good.' He stroked her hand with warm fingers.

Hope was usually so cautious with men, never feeling quite at ease with them, but sitting here with Robbie seemed right.

And then there was a shout from around the side of the building. 'Hey, Robbie, where are you? We're about to start again.'

'I suppose we'd better go in,' said Robbie with a sigh. He pulled her to her feet and they walked back towards the lights of the entrance. Hope freed her hand.

As they rounded the corner Hope saw there was quite a crowd of people, mostly young women, gathered by the steps. Then she realised why.

Claire and Luke were standing on the top step, dressed smartly in their 'going away' clothes, and Claire held her bouquet in one hand.

'Do you want me to throw it?' she was saying teasingly to the women.

'Throw it!'

'Hurry up!'

'To me!'

The calls came from all over, young and old giggling and trying to attract Claire's attention. Hope hung back, amused. She'd seen this happen in films, but never in real life.

'You have to turn your back on them,' said Luke, turning his new wife with the arm not holding his crutch. 'OK. One, two, three, throw!'

Claire made a valiant attempt to toss the bouquet of roses and lilies into the crowd behind her, but either she had a very poor aim, or she had been confused by being swung around.

Instead of going straight, the bouquet spun off to Claire's right, missing the gathering of laughing people completely, and sailing out towards Hope and Robbie.

Hope instinctively took a step backwards, not wanting to be hit, but Robbie stuck out a hand and caught the flowers by the neatly wrapped stems.

This feat was met with cheers and catcalls.

'Your turn next, brother,' shouted

Luke, grinning from ear to ear.

'Now why on earth did I do that,' muttered Robbie, trying to hand the bouquet to Hope, who hid her arms behind her back. 'You take it. I can't walk inside with a bunch of flowers.'

'No way,' said Hope firmly.

Robbie Tries To Mend Family Ties

Susie was very pleased with the way the wedding had gone. It was heart-warming to see the community enjoy themselves together. Only John Mackenzie had looked a little glum during the speeches, but even he had cheered up in the end.

Now Susie felt she needed to turn her attention back to Hope.

'We need to find Hope another job,' she said to Simon as they enjoyed their first cup of tea of the day.

'Hope needs to find herself another job, or decide what she wants to do next,' said Simon. 'It's nothing to do with you.'

'Of course it is,' said Susie, refusing to be depressed by his tone. 'I love helping people out. Steven would have been so much better off if he'd taken my advice about moving back to Scotland. I haven't given up on that yet, but I'm leaving him be for the moment.'

'If you ever persuade Steven to do something he doesn't want, I'll be surprised.' Simon even managed at small smile at the thought.

'That's the point. You've got to make people think they want it, then they do the right thing.'

'Susie, far better to let people run their own lives.'

'I only interfere if it's needed,' said Susie happily. 'And my feelings about Robbie Mackenzie and Hope are proving right. Did you see them holding hands at the end of the dance?'

'If Robbie and Hope are meant for each other, they'll sort things out themselves. People can travel, you know.'

'Mmm,' said Susie. 'You wouldn't mind if she moved back in here with us, would you?'

'Of course not. But only if that is

what she wants.'

'She could easily make enough money for her everyday expenses by taking in sewing. She's got a real talent as a dressmaker. That would mean she would be all right financially, but I've a feeling she wouldn't want to be beholden to us for accommodation.'

'She needs to get the liquidation of the shop sorted out. Once that's wound up, she can move on.'

'That's true. I think I need to talk to her about that.'

'And don't push her too hard,' said Simon. 'She strikes me as the sort of girl who likes to make up her own mind about things.'

Susie shook her head. 'She needs to accept who her family are, that's important too.'

'Why is it so important she knows about Elspeth's family? What about her dad's family?'

'There was nothing complicated there, nothing hidden. Elspeth was always happy to talk to Hope about them. We need her to be as at ease about her mother's side.'

Simon looked doubtful, but there was no time for further discussion now. She could hear the grandchildren running around downstairs and, as this was the last day of their visit, she intended to make the most of it.

★   ★   ★

Robbie's father wasn't speaking to him. He didn't know what he'd done to make things worse than usual, but he must have done something. The silent treatment was only reserved for the very worst occasions.

He put up with it all the first day after Luke and Claire's departure, but by late afternoon on the Monday he had had enough. He found his mother alone in the kitchen and asked her outright, 'What's wrong with Dad? What have I done now?'

His mother looked around cautiously, to see if they were alone. 'Well, it's not so much what you have done.'

'Huh?' Robbie pulled out a chair and sprawled back into it. He wished his mum would look at him, but she was busying herself with the pots and pans on the Rayburn. 'What on earth have I not done? I thought he would at least be pleased I helped out with the ceilidh band.'

'You were brilliant,' said his mother, flashing a smile at him over her shoulder.

'Dad obviously didn't think so. What's got into him?'

His mother gave a long sigh. She put aside the spoon she was holding and came to sit down beside him. 'It was your speech.'

'My speech?' Robbie thought he had done pretty well there. And he couldn't recall saying anything untoward about his father. 'But I never mentioned him in my speech.'

'Exactly. That's the problem. You had jokes and thanks and I don't know what, for everyone from Gran to me to

Luke, even Claire's sister, but you never said a word about your father.'

Robbie stared at her. She was right. When he thought back over his words, he hadn't made a single reference to his father. It hadn't been intentional. It just hadn't occurred to him. 'But . . . '

'He's hurt,' said his mother gently. 'Luke managed to mention him once or twice, to thank him, but even he didn't say much. You said nothing at all.'

'I didn't do it on purpose,' said Robbie. Goodness, who would ever have thought his father could be hurt, and by something like this?

'Does your father mean so little to you, you don't even think about whether you mention him or not?' His mother's expression was serious, unusual for her. 'Over the last few years I've tried not to interfere between you boys and your dad. I thought it was up to you to sort out whatever needed to be sorted out. But you just don't see it, do you? Your father loves you and it hurts him when you are so cold and distant.'

'*I'm* cold and distant?' Robbie was having difficulty taking all this in. '*I'm* the one at fault?'

'You're not the only one at fault, but you are at fault.'

'Why don't you say something to Dad about the way he is? About the constant criticism, the harping on about the least mistake?'

'As I said, I thought you should try and sort things out between you. It's not up to me to act as some kind of link between you. He and Luke have found a way of getting on. But you and he never did see eye to eye. You're too alike. But you're both grown men, do you really think it's my job to sort things out between you?'

Robbie just looked at her. She seemed very upset. Not her usual shouting and excitable upset, but a deep-down sadness.

'I just thought he didn't really care,' he said after a long silence.

'Oh, yes, he cares.'

'Then why doesn't he show it?' Robbie ran his fingers through his hair, frustrated and confused.

'Why don't you?' said his mother in return. 'Why don't you make an effort? See if he wants to go out for a pint with you?'

'But what would we talk about?' said Robbie, appalled.

'You could tell him about your work as a Countryside Ranger. Or ask his advice about how to get the farmers to co-operate with you. Or talk about your music, your friends. It doesn't all have to be arguments about the farm.'

Robbie wasn't sure it was possible to talk about anything else with his father. He wasn't at all convinced his mother's interpretation of the situation was the right one. But she looked so unhappy, and he hated to see that. Maybe he should give it a try.

After a long pause he said, 'OK, I'll suggest we go out, say after tea tonight. Do you really think he would come?'

'Not tonight. It's the village bowling

on a Monday. Maybe tomorrow?'

'I'll, er, do my best,' said Robbie. He was relieved he had at least one day's respite. An evening out with his father? Goodness, he couldn't think of many things he'd rather avoid.

'And don't, whatever you do, say it was my idea,' said his mother, rising to her feet to check once more on her cooking.

He heard his father's footsteps in the back kitchen, so he couldn't respond to that.

★   ★   ★

Hope was on her way to the Ashburys'. Susie had phoned and invited her for afternoon tea, saying she had found the photographs she had promised to show her. Hope was still torn between anger at the secrets that had been kept from her, and an increasing desire to know more about this strange family of hers.

'How's Mr Jackson?' asked Susie cheerfully as she ushered Hope inside.

'I think he really enjoyed the wedding, don't you?'

'He did enjoy it, but it tired him. He's lying down at the moment and I had real problems getting him to do his exercises today. He said his leg was sore. I wonder if I should call the doctor?'

'He never was keen on those exercises, I wouldn't worry. If he's still not right in a couple of days you can think again.'

'I'll do that,' said Hope. She followed Susie into the kitchen where a tea tray was already laid out. 'Gosh, you are organised.'

'I just need to pour the water into the teapot and we can go through.' Susie chatted on as she filled the teapot and carried the tray into the bright and airy conservatory. Hope suspected her godmother was filling any silences because she was nervous of what lay ahead.

What did lie ahead? Just looking at a few old photographs. There was nothing wrong with that, was there?

It felt quite odd to see so many pictures of her mother when she was young. She had seen plenty of pictures of her father's childhood, but the earliest picture of Elspeth had been at her wedding. Now Susie was passing her picture after picture, of Elspeth alone or with Susie, at school.

'This is your mum ready for the end-of-school dance,' said Susie. 'Now.' She took a deep breath and bent closer. 'This is your grandfather, Elspeth's dad Joseph.'

Hope peered at the black and white print. The man was slightly built and looked ill at ease before the camera, but the overriding impression was one of pride. He had one hand proudly on Elspeth's shoulder. Hope tried to work out how old he would be. Probably in his late fifties. He looked older, with what little hair he had cut very short, and a heavily lined face. She remembered Susie had said he never quite recovered from his time in the concentration camp.

'He looks nice,' she said.

'He was a lovely man. A great gardener, I told you that, didn't I? He used to smuggle handful of peas in their pods to your mother and I when we were younger.' Susie smiled reminiscently. 'He did grow a few flowers, I remember that now, although Jane didn't really approve.'

Hope examined the picture again.

'I wish it was in colour,' she said.

'There are a few snaps of the wedding in colour, I'll show you those in a minute. But even then the official ones were in black and white. Your mother insisted they couldn't afford colour. Or maybe it was your gran who insisted. I can't remember now. Look, here are some of the wedding ones.'

Hope turned her eyes to the woman who must be her grandmother. She was finding she liked her less the more she heard about her. This was the woman who had given up her own child for adoption. Who had kept the secret of her birth from Elspeth for all those years.

'Yes, that's Jane. She was very attractive, even at that age. Apparently she had been a real beauty in her youth.' Hope remembered Mrs Slater's words, saying how Hope looked like her grandmother. Was she like this tall, slender woman who held herself aloof from the crowd around her? A little pill-box hat was perched on the top of her head. It should have looked silly, but instead looked stylish.

Hope looked closer. Apart from the bride, Jane was easily the best dressed person there. Her suit fitted beautifully. The blouse beneath was of some soft material that hung in perfect pleats. She looked out of place among the cheery, crumpled crowd.

'Where on earth did she get the money for her clothes?' she asked. 'I thought you said my grandfather was an estate worker, they can't have been well off.' Hope wanted something else to dislike Jane Irving Calvert for.

For some reason Susie looked pleased by this comment. 'Oh, no, she didn't spend any money on her clothes. Jane was an expert needlewoman. I thought you knew? I've always presumed that's where you get it from. Sewing and materials were the only things that really brought Jane to life.'

Hope stared at her. She got her love of sewing from her grandmother? No!

'I never knew that.'

'I suppose sewing suited Jane. She liked to keep herself to herself and it was something she could do inside. Her dad, Matthew Irving, was said to be just the same. Jane wasn't the easiest person, but I have to say she sewed beautifully, and she could be generous with it. She made your mum's wedding dress, of course, and my bridesmaid's one. Don't you think it's lovely, with that Queen Anne neckline? It was pale pink, I'll show you on the colour snaps. And your gran altered it for me afterwards, took up the hem a bit so I could wear it for dancing. I told you, she could be kind.'

Once again the kaleidoscope of who she thought she was, what her past contained, had shifted, and she was left confused and bemused.

'You're A Good Girl, Hope'

Hope had been looking forward to her evening out with Robbie. It had been decided they would go to an early movie in Dumfries and then for a meal afterwards. Now, however, she was sure there was something wrong with Mr Jackson and she didn't think she should go.

Susie disagreed. They were discussing the situation over the phone.

'Of course you should go. I'll get his tea for him, as I promised. Simon is going to come down and we'll all eat together. He enjoys a chat with Mr Jackson. Once he's in bed Simon can go back home but if you're really worried I'm quite happy to stay at Kirkside.'

'No, he won't like that. I am grateful to you, it's just . . . I don't know, he hasn't been quite himself since the wedding and he looks a bit flushed today.'

'Simon can have a look at him when he comes down. Having a retired GP on hand can come in quite useful.'

'I suppose so . . . '

'You go and get yourself ready. You can't let Robbie down when he's gone to all that trouble.'

Hope allowed herself to be persuaded and an hour later was sitting beside Robbie in his four-by-four, heading into town. She felt shy. This was an official date, not the casual chats she had become accustomed to.

Robbie didn't seem to be quite his normal easy going self, either. She wondered if he was regretting asking her out.

'Was it difficult to get away from the farm?' she asked nervously. 'I know you have a lot to do. It's very good of you to work with your dad like this.'

'It wasn't that difficult at all,' said Robbie, frowning. 'I wasn't going to ask my dad to help, because he can be so awkward. But he suggested it himself. Weird, actually.'

'Maybe he thought you deserved some time off?'

'I doubt it. More likely he wants to check up on me, do the cows himself so he can be sure they're all right. I actually invited him out for a drink with me some time this week, but he said he didn't have the time.' Robbie looked most put out, and Hope could sympathise. What she had seen of his father, he wasn't an easy man. It was good of Robbie to invite him out.

'Maybe he appreciated the gesture?'

'Maybe. Who knows, with dad. I've given up trying to fathom him out.' But his frown remained, and Hope suspected he hadn't given up at all, he was still pondering on the problem. It was good to see someone who made an effort with their family.

The film was being shown in a small cinema on the banks of the river. Afterwards Robbie had booked a table in a restaurant in the same building.

Over the meal, they chatted about the film, a South American comedy that had been peculiar rather than funny, and about Luke and Claire who were due back in a few days time, and about the food which was delicious.

Once again, Robbie was very easy to talk to. He seemed to have recovered from whatever unease had troubled him earlier on. He took her hand as it lay on the table, listening attentively to what she said.

'Are you going to play in that ceilidh band again?' she asked him, wanting to learn more about him. 'I didn't realise you could play so well. I mean, I know you said you played a bit, but that was amazing.'

'It was a good job I'd been practising, wasn't it?' he said with a grin. 'It's something I've always loved doing, playing the fiddle. I'd kind of wondered about getting back into a band, but it won't be *Abhainn*. They don't need a second fiddler, although they've said they'll call on me if they ever need a stand-in, which I suppose is a compliment.'

'They should have paid you,' said Hope, laughing.

'Actually, they offered, but I thought it better if they reduced their price. Anyway, I couldn't take payment for playing at my brother's wedding, could I? Even if my father probably does think that is what happened.'

His frown returned. Hope wondered why he hadn't just told his father the truth, but decided that would have been too straightforward. She sought for a change of subject to distract him.

'I'm going to need to do something to earn a bit of money myself,' she said. She began to tell him about the dressmaking jobs she had taken on, and how much she was enjoying them.

'But like your music, I don't think I could make a living from it. And anyway, I'm not trained as a dress-maker.'

'Sounds to me as though you are as good as. Claire thought you were better than the woman they paid to do the bridesmaids' dresses. She was very impressed.'

Hope blushed, pleased and embarrassed. 'That was nothing, honestly.'

'But you enjoy doing it, don't you? Why don't you take on a bit more and see how it goes?'

'I don't know.' Hope had never considered it seriously. 'I'd need to set myself up properly, have my own studio and so on.'

'And would you like to do that?'

Hope shrugged. 'I'm not sure.' She was enjoying sewing to demand more than she had expected. Previously she had only made things for herself or occasionally for close friends. She hadn't seen this as a marketable skill. 'I thought I was more interested in fabrics. I never intended getting into the design and sewing side.' She smiled at the thought of the pleasure she had had, setting up her lovely shop. 'It is such fun, sourcing materials, providing the right ones for the right people. I just loved looking at the shelves and shelves of fabric. I suppose that sounds stupid, doesn't it? Anyway, that didn't work out.'

'It must have been awful, your friend disappearing, letting you down like that.' Robbie stroked her hand gently, his sympathy so sincere she found herself telling him more about what had happened. And about how Amy had now been found, and how instead of being relieved she just felt more confused.

'My solicitor wants me to press charges against her. But I can't do that, can I?'

'Why not?' Robbie didn't seem judgemental, just interested.

'She was my friend.'

'But if she stole from you she wasn't really your friend, was she? And she didn't just steal from you.'

Hope looked down, embarrassed. 'In the end, nobody else lost out.'

'How was that? I don't understand. I thought you said she'd taken everything, left you with lots of debts.'

'She did. She left the business with huge debts.' She sighed. She knew he was going to think she was stupid, like everyone else did. 'But I paid everything off, from my own money.'

'Goodness. Did you have to do that? Has it left you penniless?'

'I didn't have to, legally. We had a limited liability partnership which meant I wasn't legally responsible for the business debts. But I felt responsible. So I paid them.'

He looked at her for a long time in silence. 'That was a very noble thing to do.'

'What?' She was amazed. Her solicitor and accountant had thought she was crazy. She hadn't even explained the details to Simon and Susie, she knew they too would have advised her not to do it. And now Robbie sounded approving.

'You don't think I'm mad? That I should have let other people suffer and kept the money for myself?'

'Not if you felt you shouldn't. And

you're not that kind of person, are you?'

Now that he was taking her side, Hope felt she had to explain what a fool she had been. 'But it was my mother's money, money she left me to set myself up in life. That's what she thought she was doing. And I just wasted it.' She still felt guilty about that. She didn't regret giving the money away, but she was sorry she had let her mother down.

'Your mother must have brought you up to be the way you are. Maybe she would have understood?'

Hope thought that over. It was a new idea. Her mother had always been careful with money. She had had to be, bringing up a child on her small widow's pension and her part-time earnings. But she had been scrupulously honest in her financial dealings.

She wondered if the way her mother was about money stemmed from her own childhood. She imagined money had been tight at Cleughbrae. In answer to Robbie's question, she nodded and said, 'You know, I think she might have understood. My mother never liked to see anyone struggling.'

'Well, there you are then. It's just a shame it has left you without a nest egg. Do you think there is any chance you could get any of the money back from your so-called friend?'

'No,' said Hope. She decided, at that moment, she wouldn't even try. It was over. Best to leave the past behind and move on. 'Actually, it didn't take all my money, just most of it. I'm not completely poverty stricken.' She didn't want him to think she was seeking sympathy.

'That's good,' said Robbie smiling at her warmly. 'You're better off than I am then. I thought coming to live back at home was a good idea. Mum was keen and I thought it would let me save up so I could get a place of my own. But the longer I stay at the farm the more I think I was wrong. If it was possible I'd move out right now.'

'Your mum would hate that,' said Hope immediately.

'What about my father? I'm sure he'd love it. They're both perfectly fine about Luke and Claire moving into the little bungalow at the edge of the village.'

'That's different,' said Hope immediately. 'They're getting married. They'll want to start their new life in a place of their own.'

'I suppose,' said Robbie. He looked at her in a new way, as though something had changed, although she couldn't imagine what. 'Yes,' he said, raising her hand suddenly to his lips and kissing her fingers. 'Yes, you're probably right.'

Hope wasn't sure if she was pleased or disappointed when the waiter came up to see if they wanted dessert and Robbie released her hand to take the menu.

★   ★   ★

It had been a lovely evening. Everything about it was perfect. The strange little movie, the meal, Robbie's company.

199

They didn't stay out too late. Much as Hope was enjoying herself, a little part of her mind was still worrying about Mr Jackson, and soon after ten they set off home.

'We could do this again sometime?' suggested Robbie as he drew up before Kirkside.

'I'd like that. I . . . ' Hope paused and looked about.

Something was wrong. There were too many lights on in the house, practically every downstairs room was lit. And Simon Ashbury's car was still here. As she peered around, Hope saw a second vehicle which she didn't recognise.

She jumped out of the car without another word and ran up the steps, pushing open the heavy wooden door.

Susie came hurrying out of the kitchen.

'Hope, my dear, I'm so glad you're here. I couldn't decide whether to phone you but I didn't want to disturb your evening . . . '

'What's wrong? Is Mr Jackson all right?'

'He's not too well. Simon was starting to worry about his temperature and we decided to get the on-call doctor to come and have a look. Mr Jackson was quite awkward about it, I don't know how you've coped with him, it's not easy to get him to do something he doesn't want, is it? But it's a good thing we went ahead. They think it's a blood clot and an ambulance is on its way. He needs to have it dealt with as soon as possible.'

'A blood clot? But surely . . . ' Hope had read all the notes about what to do after an operation like Mr Jackson's. She had tried to follow the instructions. She remembered what the symptoms were. A high temperature. Pain in the calf or leg. Should she have realised?

'Can I go and see him?'

'The doctor's still with him. Such a young man, they seem to be scarcely out of their teens these days . . . Ah, here they are.'

201

Simon Ashbury and a dark-haired man who didn't look particularly young to Hope, appeared from Mr Jackson's bedroom. She waited only long enough for them to confirm what Susie had told her, and then went in to see the old man herself.

He was lying propped up on his pillows, looking dazed. He didn't turn his head as she approached.

Hope took his hand, which was very hot. 'I'm sorry I wasn't here,' she said softly. 'You'll be right as rain as soon as they get you to hospital.'

'Ah, you're back.' He paused. 'Didn't want to spoil your evening.'

'My evening doesn't matter! It's getting you well that counts.'

'I'm an old man, Hope. Don't take on so.'

Hope could feel tears welling up in her eyes. He sounded like he had given up. 'You've got to fight this,' she said, desperately. 'Now they've identified the problem you'll be fine.'

'I'm very tired,' he said so quietly she

could hardly hear. The words made her shiver. She remembered her mother saying that, near the end.

'You'll be fine,' she said again, squeezing his thin fingers. 'I'll come to the hospital so you're not on your own.'

'No. Stay with Lucy.' A pause. 'You're a good girl, Hope.'

Sounds outside heralded the arrival of the ambulance and there was no time for further conversation. Lucy stood with her shaggy head pressed against Hope's leg as Mr Jackson was transferred to a stretcher. The old man had placed a shaking hand on the dog's rough coat for a moment before they took him away.

As the ambulance departed Hope knelt down beside Lucy and buried her face in the long grey hair. Just for a moment, she couldn't bear to think. She had lost her father, and then her mother. She realised Mr Jackson was now so important to her he could almost be family. She couldn't be going to lose him, too, could she?

Susie and Simon and even Robbie offered to sit with her, but she assured them she was fine and eventually they left. Robbie held her tightly as he kissed her goodbye, but she couldn't think about him now. She could only think about Mr Jackson and how she had let him down.

★ ★ ★

Hope didn't sleep at all that night. She took Lucy up to her bedroom, much to the dog's confusion, and lay in the darkness, not even closing her eyes. She dropped one hand to the side of the bed to rest on the warm head of the bearded collie. It was the only comfort she could find.

As soon as the grey light of morning began to show at the window she rose. Wrapping herself in a dressing gown, she went downstairs to let Lucy out and put on the kettle for tea. Was it too early to phone the hospital? She had no idea, but she was going to try.

Surprisingly, after a number of delays, Hope was put through to the High Dependency Unit. She explained to the staff nurse she was Mr Jackson's carer and was told he had come through the emergency thrombectomy with no apparent ill effects. They were hopeful there would be no long term damage.

When she put the phone down she burst into tears. Mr Jackson had a very good chance of coming through. Lucy nudged her leg, not understanding but keen to help. Hope slid to her knees on the floor and flung her arms around the dog.

Hope had a shower and walked Lucy around to the Ashburys' to tell them the news. Despite her lack of sleep, by the time she returned to Kirkside she was bursting with energy. It was still too early to go in to the hospital, but she had to do something.

Her eye fell on the box of photos that Susie had pushed into her arms all those days ago. Did she have the energy

— and the courage — to look at them now?

She made herself a mug of coffee and carried the box to the kitchen table.

The box contained more than just pictures of her mother she had already seen. This was a whole family photograph collection. Hope turned over the curling black and white pictures. Some had names written on the back, occasionally there were even dates, but mostly there were just faces staring fixedly at the camera. It was unnerving. Were these people her family?

Gradually she began to sort them out. She found a pen and paper and began to make notes. She knew who her grandparents were now. Jane Calvert nee Irving and Joseph Calvert. She examined them on the pictures Susie had shown her and then worked backwards. Here was Jane and Joseph's wedding picture, just the two of them, wearing dark suits and even darker expressions. Had Jane told Joseph by this time what she had done to his child?

And going further back was a picture of Joseph in uniform, with his hair neatly parted and his face pale. And then one or two of children, always boys. These must be the Calvert boys, Joseph and his brothers.

One thing was clear. The Calvert family had been a happy one. The adults might stare solemnly at the camera, but the children giggled and posed. They had arms around each other's shoulders, leant happily against an adult's leg. Yes, this was a family having fun. She wrote down the names of the boys: Tom, Charlie, Michael, Norman and Joseph, the baby. On one photograph it was marked 'Joe, Lizzie and children'. So her grandmother, Joseph's mother, had been Lizzie. She wrote those names down, too, and found she had the beginning of a family tree.

But why was there nothing of the Irvings? Didn't Jane's family take photographs?

Then, almost at the bottom of the

box, she found a framed picture of a beautiful toddler with long ringlets and dark eyes. This had been taken by a professional photographer. She turned it over. *Jane Elspeth Irving 1908*. At last, some record of Jane. Her parents had prized her, too, had had her photograph taken and had framed it. She really was a pretty little thing. Hope examined it for a long time.

There was no other record of the Irvings. Hope realised she didn't even know if Jane had been an only child, although she presumed so. Hope found she wanted to know more. The only problem was, how could she find out?

* * *

Hope hadn't realised how fond she had grown of Mr Jackson. Yes, he was crotchety and difficult. He didn't always like to chat and he could be fussy and critical. But he was interested in her, too, and she in him. He might be well into his eighties but his mind and

208

his sense of humour were as lively as those of a much younger man. He was, quite simply, good company, and Hope missed him.

She still felt very guilty about having let him fall ill. Despite everyone's assurances, she was sure if she had been a little more observant, a little bossier, she could have made things better. But most of all she was relieved he was recovering, and desperate to have him back home.

It made her think about the future. She couldn't stay with him forever, she knew that. He wouldn't want it and nor did she. But did she really want to move far away, not to see him for months at a time, if ever?

She tried not to think what role Robbie Mackenzie might play in these plans. She hardly knew him, really. He had been very supportive after Mr Jackson was rushed to hospital, but he hadn't pushed her to go out with him again. He had probably changed his mind. Which was absolutely fine. She wasn't looking for a serious relation-ship. If he wanted to be just friends, she was perfectly happy with that.

Her musings on this topic were not helped by Susie, who popped by or phoned at least every other day and, somehow, managed to mention Robbie every time.

'Such a nice boy,' she was saying, on her latest visit. 'Imagine him giving up his own job to help out his father like that. That's what I call real family feeling.'

'Yes,' said Hope, hunting around for another subject to distract her god-mother. 'Did I tell you that Sarah phoned? She seems very pleased with the ballgown I made for her. I posted it up last week and she says it fits perfectly, which is lucky.'

'More skill than luck, I'd say,' said Susie. 'She told me she was delighted with it. And mentioned a couple of her friends might be getting in touch about a special outfit for Christmas. That would be good news, wouldn't it?'

'I'm flattered, of course,' said Hope. 'But I don't know how practical it is, with them being in Edinburgh'

'You've got a car and no doubt so have they. It's only an hour-and-a-half away. And you did promise to go and visit Sarah. Once Mr Jackson is home and settled perhaps you could schedule a visit in along with a session of fittings?'

Hope shook her head doubtfully. 'Maybe. Now I need to take Lucy for a quick walk before I head over to the hospital. Do you want to come with me?'

'Yes, why not. You remember we said we might go and have another look at Cleughbrae? Why don't we do that?'

She had an intentness to her expression that made Hope immediately wary. She did want to go and have another look at Cleughbrae. But not with Susie, and not today. Susie had a way of making you see things her way, and that was no longer what Hope wanted.

'I don't think we've time for that today,' she said firmly, and was relieved when Susie didn't insist.

* * *

Robbie decided it was time he sorted himself out. It felt as though his life had been on hold for weeks, months even. He had to get back to his own job and start thinking about the future. He had helped out the family by taking Luke's place on the farm, but Luke and Claire were home now and it was time to move on.

Robbie had phoned his boss, Jamie, to arrange a date for starting back at work, and the older man had suggested he come in for a chat so they could plan the next few months. That was what Robbie needed, someone who believed in him.

He felt almost cheerful as he parked outside the estate offices. Sulwath Estates owned thousands of acres in the Southern Uplands of Scotland, but you wouldn't have known it from the modest buildings here. That was one of the things Robbie liked about the organisation. They put their money into things that mattered — the countryside — not into fancy offices.

He found Jamie sitting behind his desk, frowning at the computer screen. He was a tall man with very short hair and a weather-beaten complexion, who always looked slightly ill at ease when not outdoors.

He rose with relief and shook Robbie's hand. 'Good to see you. Everything all right at home? Grab yourself a wee coffee. There's something I want to discuss with you.'

Robbie took a seat. For a while they chatted about the projects he had been working on before his extended leave. The ranger-led walks had been very popular, but they would tail off now the winter was approaching. Jamie seemed impressed with the way he had got many of the local farmers to work with the estate on land management, especially the regeneration of indigenous forest.

'I'm keen to get on with the bug survey as soon as I'm back,' said Robbie.

'Ah, yes,' said Jamie, rubbing his chin. 'I was hoping young Susan would take that on. I don't think you'll have much time for any hands-on involvement.'

Robbie frowned. He'd been looking forward to doing the survey. What on earth did Jamie have in store for him? Maybe he hadn't been pulling his weight as well as he had thought, maybe they weren't happy with his work. After over a month of being constantly in his father's company, that was all too easy to believe.

'We've been having a bit of a reorganisation,' said Jamie, watching him carefully. 'There's so much going on in conservation and land management these days that no one can keep an eye on the whole estate any more. We've decided to split it into two regions, east and west.'

'Ah,' said Robbie, to show he was listening. He could see the sense of that. The estate stretched from Nithsdale in the west right through to the Scottish Borders. It wasn't just the size that made it difficult to manage as one entity, it was also the very disparate land uses.

'I've been wanting to do it for some time,' said Jamie. 'But it's taken a while to talk the laird round. He's finally agreed to give it a one year trial. I'm to carry on in my job, but concentrating on the east of the region. And we're looking for a Senior Ranger to take the lead in the west area. Your name immediately came to mind and we wondered if you'd consider taking it on, for one year initially.'

Robbie didn't need to consider. 'Yes!' he said, grinning from ear to ear. 'I mean, I'd need to know more about what you'd expect from me, but basically, I'd be delighted.'

Some good news, at last! He spent

the next hour talking over the options with Jamie, and when he left the office felt a foot taller than when he had gone in. This would mean more money, which was always welcome, or course, but most of all it was recognition. And the chance to put a few of the ideas he had into practice without always having to seek approval first. And the chance to train up juniors just the way he knew they should be trained. And to introduce more walks, winter ones this time, the possibilities were endless.

As he drove back to St. Ann's Bridge he knew there was one person he wanted to share this news with. Hope McIlroy. He hadn't see much of her recently. She had been so caught up with Mr Jackson, and he hadn't been in the best of moods, knowing how useless his father thought him to be. It was hard to press someone to go out with you, when you were a failure.

But he wasn't a failure any more! It was amazing what a little bit of appreciation could do. He called straight round to Kirkside, but unfortunately there was no one there.

★　★　★

One good thing had come from Mr Jackson's latest problems. His son Andrew had finally arranged to visit from Australia. He and the younger of his three grown up children were due to arrive at the weekend.

'I've got everything ready for when Andrew arrives,' said Hope when she visited Mr Jackson in hospital a couple of days before he was due home. 'They're hiring a car in Glasgow and should arrive early Sunday afternoon.' She had handled most of the communication with Andrew, as phone calls to and from the hospital weren't easy. Previously she had been rather annoyed with the man, on his father's behalf. Why hadn't he taken more interest, visited sooner? Now she had got to know him better and realised he had problems of his own. His wife suffered from poor health and he was self-employed which made it difficult for him to get away.

'It'll be good to see him, I can't deny it,' said Mr Jackson. 'But don't you go putting yourself to too much trouble. It's not your job to look after visitors as well as Lucy and me.'

'I don't mind,' said Hope. She liked it when Mr Jackson's old impatience showed through.

'The boy he's bringing with him, Mark, he must be about your age. He should be able to help out, not need looking after.'

'There was one thing I wondered.' Hope hesitated. 'If you've got family staying, maybe you'd rather be on your own with them?' She hadn't been sure how to put this. She didn't want Mr Jackson to be offended. And, sure enough, he was starting to scowl.

She hurried on. 'I could easily stay with the Ashburys for a while, give you some time alone together.'

'Rubbish,' said Mr Jackson firmly. 'I

need you. I'm not having Andrew doing my washing and helping me in and out of bed. And he wouldn't have a clue what to do with all these blessed pills and potions you put out for me.'

'I'm happy to stay, if you're sure?' Hope was touched that he wanted her. 'But you know I will have to move out at some point. Soon you'll be perfectly capable of looking after yourself. It's a waste of your money to keep paying me, and besides it's not good for you to rely on someone else.'

She was worried that Mr Jackson might be put out by this plain speaking but he just patted her hand. 'We'll think about that in a wee while, shall we? With the fuss the doctors are making I can't see them being happy for me to be on my own just yet.'

Hope nodded, willing to allow the subject to drop for now. She began to tell him about Lucy's insistence on sleeping in Mr Jackson's room even though he wasn't there, and then a few tidbits of gossip from the village.

He tried to pretend he wasn't interested in gossip, but he couldn't help himself. 'So young Robbie is giving up on his father and going back to his own work, is he?'

'I don't think you can say he's giving up. Luke is home now and almost fully recovered.'

'Hmmph. And have you been seeing much of Robbie yourself? I hear my grandson's been asking about you, asking his dad to find out if you're single and pretty, but I told him you were spoken for.'

Hope opened her mouth to protest, but found she was speechless. She was used to Susie being pushy, but not Mr Jackson. She cleared her throat, hoping she wasn't blushing. 'Robbie and I are just good friends.'

'Hmmph,' said Mr Jackson again. He closed his eyes and lay back on his pillows.

Hope was relieved. She didn't want to discuss Robbie with him. After seeing very little of him for almost a fortnight he had phoned and invited her to go for a picnic the very next day. He told her about his promotion and said he wanted to celebrate. Hope had been pleased to accept the invitation, but then wondered if she should have been less eager. She didn't want him to think she was someone who could be picked up or dropped as it suited him. Was that the kind of person Robbie was? She really didn't know him very well.

'I Couldn't Possibly Buy It'

'Where are we going?' Hope asked Robbie as they set off in his Land Rover. It was October and not really her idea of a good time of year to picnic. She hoped she had dressed warmly enough for the cool, misty day.

'Remember I once told you about the upland bogs?' Robbie turned to smile at her.

Hope was surprised he remembered that brief conversation so long ago. 'Yes. But actually, I didn't know what they were.'

'That's what I figured. So I thought I'd go and show you. I need to check out the area we're visiting for a possible project at work and I thought you might like to come along.'

Although Hope had warned herself

to keep a distance from Robbie, she found it was impossible to do so. He was so relaxed, such good fun to be with. He explained how important the wetlands were for wildlife and with an occasional helping hand from him she found herself walking for miles across the deserted hill.

When they stopped for the picnic they sat close together on the small blanket and ate their sandwiches and fruit in silence. Hope was pleased her newly acquired walking boots were standing up to the outing. She was almost too hot and took off her multi-coloured hat to help her cool down.

She waved it around at the land that fell in gentle waves of green and brown before them. 'It's wonderful up here. I would never have thought of a picnic at this time of year, but it's brilliant.'

'So you thought it was a crazy idea, did you?' Robbie grinned at her.

'I was sure you were tough enough for it, I just wasn't sure I was.'

'Of course you are. You're very

tough.' He took her hand for a moment and looked at it. 'Although you do look so delicate. Don't you think you should put your hat and gloves back on? The wind up here can be very chilling.'

He took her hand as they walked back down to the Land Rover and began to tell her more about his work and how much he was enjoying the new job.

'Better than working for you dad?' she teased.

He flinched and then managed a smile as he said, 'Definitely better than that. I think we just about came through it still on speaking terms, but it was a close thing.'

'Did you ever go out for that drink with him?'

'No, we never did.'

Robbie sighed and they were silent for a while. When he began to speak again he had turned the conversation to her, and he seemed so interested she found herself telling him about all the photographs she had been looking through, particularly the ones of Cleughbrae. Without realising it, she found herself agreeing to go and visit the house again, this time with him. It was about time she got over her silly aversion to the place, wasn't it?

★   ★   ★

Hope had wanted to go back to the house where her mother had grown up for a while now, but something made her hold back. She changed the subject whenever Susie tried to speak to her about it. Robbie was different. He wouldn't push her into anything she didn't want. His hand was warm and comforting in hers and the track down to the house no longer looked so intimidating.

'I haven't been down here for years,' he said cheerfully. 'I was friendly with a boy who lived here when we were in primary school, but he didn't stay long.'

'Susie said it's owned by the local estate and was used by them to house workers. I think there have been a fair few families passing through.'

They rounded the corner and came out of the trees. There was the little house looking isolated in the expanse of over-long grass.

'Mmm. Doesn't exactly look cared for, does it?' said Robbie. But he didn't seem put off.

The house was just as small as she remembered, with dirty windows and moss growing in the gutters. But she could see, now, that it could be quite a pretty place. Over the front door, which stood out from the house in a little porch, was a very fancy stone frontispiece. And although the paint was peeling off the door itself, it was solid, with an attractive heavy brass handle.

'It could do with a lick of paint, but it's not bad, is it?' said Robbie. 'A bit isolated, of course, but some people like that.'

'When my grandfather grew up here,' said Hope slowly, forcing herself to say the unfamiliar words, 'He was one of five children. I suppose it would have been pretty lively then.'

'Not to mention crowded,' said Robbie with a grin. 'But I suppose that was usual in those days. Do you want to have a look inside?'

They had circled the house once, and now he drew a key from his pocket. It was an old-fashioned iron key, at least four inches in length, and seemed entirely fitting for the solid old door.

'Where did you get that?'

Robbie patted his nose, as though he wasn't going to tell her, then laughed. 'It was easy. I mentioned to Mum we were coming to have a look around here. She said Dad had been talking to the estate factor and they're thinking about putting the place on the market. That being the case, I asked if it'd be OK to look around, and here we are.'

'You're not thinking of buying it, are you?' Hope looked around with new eyes. Would someone their age actually want to live here? It was so secluded, so run down ... and yet there was something appealing about it. It had character.

'Not seriously,' said Robbie easily. 'Although with the promotion I told you about I might be able to think about buying somewhere of my own, fairly soon.' He grinned at her and she smiled back.

The heavy door led into a tiny, square porch, and they opened a second glass door that took them into a dimly lit hallway. There were three doors opening off this, and a staircase straight ahead.

'Kitchen at the back, I presume,' said Robbie, waving in that direction. 'Sitting room on one side of the front door. Yes, this would be it. Nice fireplace. And then one bedroom down here.'

They made their way through the rooms. Once their eyes grew accustomed to the light, they could see well enough. The rooms weren't as small as Hope had assumed from outside. They were plainly decorated, but the deep skirting boards and cornices made them rather quaint.

Hope tried to picture her mother here, and failed. 'I wonder what it was like in the fifties and sixties,' she said.

'The main rooms wouldn't be much different. The kitchen looks like it was fitted in the seventies. I wonder when the bathroom was put in.' Robbie peered at the functional décor, the black-sided bath and institutional white tiles. 'Looks a bit bleak, doesn't it?'

Hope smiled faintly. 'It was probably quite a luxury, when it was first installed.'

She thought of the photographs she had seen of the Calvert family. Mostly they had been outside in the fields, but one or two had been in this very kitchen. Before the cupboards had been fitted it had been big enough for a kitchen table. It looked like it had been a happy, family kitchen then. Maybe not so happy, when her mother grew up here?

'My grandmother was apparently a very good cook,' she said. 'My grandfather grew loads in the garden and my grandmother made it into jams and chutneys and things.'

'Is that right? I hadn't heard that. But my mum remembers talk of her sewing. She used to take in jobs from the village. She had a little upstairs room all set up for that. Shall we go and look?'

Hope nodded. When she reached the top of the stairs she felt breathless, and it wasn't because of the steep steps.

Up here was the perfect sewing room. There were skylights facing north and south so it was very light.

'It's brilliant,' said Hope softly, looking around. It was bare now except for a dull brown carpet and some fitted shelves, but she could imagine it with a long table under one of the windows, a sewing machine under the other . . .

'It'd be cold in winter,' said Robbie. 'It's a bit on the chilly side now. No central heating.'

Hope supposed he was right, but that didn't interest her. It was the sense of connection she felt. She could almost be Jane, sitting quietly here in this peaceful room, working with her fabrics.

'It's a lovely place,' she said, following Robbie reluctantly back down the stairs.

'So it's not as gloomy as you thought?'

'No. It's not. It's really — not bad.' Suddenly Hope could picture her mother here. It would have been spic and span, everything in its place. Maybe a little too quiet for a single child of elderly parents. But really, it wouldn't have been bad.

They went back outside and Robbie locked the door behind him. Hope realised that she was cold, not surprising on a grey autumn day, and she was glad when Robbie put an arm around her. They stood looking back at the little building.

'There's something my mother said I

should tell you,' said Robbie.

She glanced up at him, alerted by the serious tone in his voice. The breeze blew the dark curls back from his face. He looked at the house, not her.

'There was apparently a special arrangement made when the house was sold, around the time of your grandmother's death. She knew your mother wouldn't want to live here but she must have hoped someone else in the family might eventually take an interest. It was sold to the estate on the proviso that if it was ever put up for resale, Jane's descendants would have the first right of refusal.'

He was silent and Hope tried to make sense of his words. 'And that means?'

'Before it goes on the open market, it has to be offered for sale to the family. At the going rate, of course, but I understand the estate are quite keen to get it off their hands, so they wouldn't be asking too much.'

'And the only member of Jane's

family left is — me.' Now Hope was sure she knew what Susie had wanted to tell her. She stared and stared at the little house and as she did so a pale sun came out from behind the clouds and lit up the clearing. The stonework shone red. It was as though it was a sign.

'I couldn't possibly buy it,' said Hope quickly. 'I don't have the money and I'm not planning on staying in St. Ann's Bridge and . . . ' There were lots of other reasons why this made no sense at all, she just couldn't think of them all just now.

'You don't need to decide yet,' said Robbie. 'Come on, you're shivering. Why don't we head back and get a coffee?'

As they walked back up the road, Robbie gave a long sigh and then said, his voice serious, 'There's something else I should tell you.'

Hope glanced at him, immediately worried. This sounded personal. 'Yes?'

'I've got to go away on Monday. It's a

training course for work, down in Wales and it lasts two weeks. Initially it wasn't supposed to be until after the New Year, but yesterday they phoned to say they have a vacancy on the course that starts on Monday and my boss is keen for me to take it.'

Hope was silent for a moment. She hated the idea of not seeing him for two whole weeks, but it could have been worse. She had feared he was about to say he didn't want to see her again. She swallowed. That was just too awful to think about. She said brightly, 'It's good your boss is keen to send you on training courses.'

'I'll miss you,' he said. 'But no doubt you'll be busy with Mr Jackson's family arriving. I'll try to phone.'

'That would be good,' said Hope. She wanted to say she would miss him too, but it seemed so forward. By the time she had plucked up the courage, the moment had passed.

★ ★ ★

Robbie had a couple of hours spare on Sunday morning and decided it was about time he did some serious fiddle practice. His bedroom at Holm Farm was on the ground floor at the back of the house so he wasn't likely to disturb anyone. *Abhainn* had asked him to play with them at a special event in a few weeks time so he had better get stuck in.

He was in an excellent mood. One week into his new job and he was loving it. Even better, things were going well with Hope McIlroy. She had coped splendidly with the visit to her mother's old house. She had even agreed to go out with him again one evening during the week. Today she was busy with the arrival of Mr Jackson's son and grandson so it was an ideal time to get back into his music. It was a pain he had to go away on this course, but the two weeks would fly by, wouldn't they?

He began to work his way through some new material *Abhainn* had given him and was so lost in joy of them he almost dropped his bow when he heard someone clearing their throat right behind him.

He swung round to find his father standing at his shoulder.

'I knocked. You didn't hear me.' This might have been meant as an apology.

'I was well away with the music.' Robbie paused and when his father remained silent he said, 'Did you want me? Or was I making too much noise?'

'The music's fine. Nice to hear you playing again.'

Robbie waited. After the compliment there was bound to be a criticism.

'I don't know if I ever said, it was good of you to help out the band at the wedding.'

Robbie wondered if he was hearing things. His father hurried on, 'I was, er, thinking about going to the Market Inn for a pint before lunch. I wondered if you'd like to come.'

Robbie had been resting the fiddle on his shoulder. Now he let it drop to his side and stared. His father was being nice to him. Suggesting pleasure rather than work? And inviting him, Robbie, to go along?

'Is Luke going?' he asked. It was the only explanation he could think of. They had been invited a couple of times to have a Sunday lunch with Luke and Claire. Maybe these family events were going to become routine.

'No. I don't know what Luke's doing. I thought you and I could have a drink, before you go off gallivanting again. But if you don't want to that's fine.'

It sounded like his dad had already changed his mind and Robbie was tempted to let him. What on earth would they talk about? But he couldn't refuse when his dad had made so much effort.

'That sounds, er, good. Is it OK with Mum?'

'She says, as long as we're back for one-thirty.'

'Well, that's, er, great then.'

His father raised an arm as though to

slap him on the shoulder in the friendly way Robbie had seem him use occasionally with Luke. Then he hesitated and let his arm fall. 'I'll let you finish your practice.'

To begin with, conversation was as difficult as Robbie had feared. Any discussion of the farm was bound to end in argument. They managed a couple of sentences about how well Luke and Claire had settled into their new house. What were they supposed to talk about next?

Whilst his father was at the bar collecting their drinks, Robbie searched his mind for something to say. He could do this.

'I met up with someone last week who knows you. He farms up by St. Mary's Loch. He's an old fellow but spritely on his feet.'

His father looked interested for the first time since they had left home. 'I mind who you mean. Cannae think of his name just now but, he was a great friend of Uncle Arthur's. Runs a big hill farm up there, doesn't he? How's the farm doing?'

'They put quite a lot of it under woodland, I suppose that saves him some work . . . ' Robbie found the conversation flowed after that. It seemed it was fine to talk about farming, as long as they didn't discuss Holm Farm. And his father even seemed interested in the work Robbie was doing, how he got on with the old hill farmers.

It was way after half-one when they arrived back at the farm, but his mother didn't complain. She smiled happily to see them chatting together. Robbie could guess whose idea it had been for them to go out for a drink. But, amazingly, it had worked out well, so he didn't really mind.

★   ★   ★

Hope was taking Lucy for one of her slow walks. She had decided to go down to the graveyard. Mr Jackson's grandson had offered to go with her, but fortunately his father had wanted to take him off to see an old acquaintance. The younger Jacksons were very pleasant, but she had the feeling that Mark wanted to spend more time with her than she did with him, which made her uncomfortable.

She took a notebook with her. She had been meaning to do this for a while. To see if she could trace all those supposed ancestors who were buried there. With Robbie's words about the possible ownership of Cleughbrae still ringing in her ears, she felt now was the time to do it.

Initially she began to look for Calvert gravestones. She found one or two. The one that made her pause was a simple stone erected in memory of *Elizabeth Calvert, daughter of Joseph and Elizabeth Calvert, who had died in 1903, aged 2 years. Safe with God.* This must have been her grandfather, Joseph's, sister. The only girl in the family, who had died so young. There had been no mention of her in Susie's reminiscences — was this yet another secret? Hope read the gravestone a number of times. Joseph Senior and Lizzie were buried in the same grave. They must never have forgotten their little daughter. For some reason this made Hope want to cry.

Without really meaning to, she found herself tracing the Irving family. She found a Jane Davidson Irving, who must be Hope's great-grandmother. She had died young. Working out the dates, Hope reckoned she had died when her daughter, the Jane who had gone to Glasgow to hide the birth of her daughter, had not yet been in her teens. What had it been like, being brought up by your father in the 1920s and 30s?

The father, Matthew, had lived a long life. He was the one someone had referred to as reclusive. Hope bent to read his gravestone, the words added on below those recording the death of his wife. Matthew, it seemed, had died in

1953. He had been living at School Cottage in St. Ann's Bridge. And he had been a tailor.

Hope shook her head in amazement. Was this where it came from, her fascination with sewing? Her grandmother, the stern and beautiful Jane, had been a very competent seamstress. And Jane's own father had been a tailor. Somehow, that pleased Hope. This was her family and she was beginning to feel a connection with them.

When she returned to Kirkside she showed Mr Jackson the notes she had made. He had encouraged her more than once to seek out her roots.

'I knew you'd find them,' he said, nodding his domed head. 'You're having fun, aren't you?'

'I suppose I am. More than I would ever have thought.' Hope poured tea for them both from the pink Wedgewood teapot. 'You must have known some of them. My great-grandfather, Matthew Irving, only died in the 1950s. Do you remember him?'

'Aye, I do. Secretive little man he was, lived in one of the cottages up by the school.'

'It says on his gravestone he was a tailor.'

Mr Jackson nodded approvingly, as though she had just passed a test. 'That's right. I believe he did a lot of sewing for the village at one time. He was too old for that when I knew him. His daughter had taken it on by then. You couldn't easily buy ready-made clothes in those days. You either had to make your own or pay a tailor.'

Hope liked the idea of that. People wouldn't have had so many garments, but what they did have would have been specially made for them. And from the evidence she had seen of Jane's skills, they would have been good.

'He was apparently not so well liked, old Matthew,' said Mr Jackson musingly, putting a dampener on these happy thoughts. 'I mind my father had something against him although I can't remember what. Maybe he was different when his wife was alive, but that was before my time. Why don't you go and ask Mrs Slater what she can remember? She might be well into her nineties but she's still sharp. I'm sure she'd be happy to talk to you.'

★ ★ ★

The last person Hope expected to see walking across the gravel to the front door of Kirkside was Amy Jones. Andrew and Mark had taken Mr Jackson for a shopping trip to Dumfries. Hope was upstairs when she heard the footsteps and she looked out of the landing window. Her heart had leapt at the thought it might be Robbie, which was ridiculous as he was in Wales. When she saw Amy she really didn't know what to think.

She heard the old-fashioned bell ring and still she didn't move. What could her former friend possibly have to say that Hope would want to hear? She had hoped that part of her life was over.

The doorbell rang again and with a sigh she went down to answer it.

Amy was a short, slightly plump girl with golden curls. Her taste in clothes used to tend towards low necks and very tight mini skirts, but today she looked oddly muted. She wore a black knitted dress over lilac leggings. Her expression was tense.

'Hello.' Hope stood on the doorstep above her former business partner. She didn't know what to say to her.

'Hi. Can I come in?'

Hope kept her hand on the door. 'How did you find me?'

'It wasn't easy. You'd changed your mobile.'

'I couldn't afford the contract,' said Hope bluntly.

Amy looked down at that and then took a breath and continued, 'I got in touch with the accountant who was . . . winding up our business. He wouldn't tell me where you were except you were a long way away. Then I remembered your Auntie Susie in Scotland and made a lucky guess.'

Hope pressed her lips together. It would be just like Susie to encourage Amy to visit, she probably hoped for a touching reconciliation.

'I suppose you'd better come in,' she said ungraciously. She led the way to the kitchen and put the kettle on to boil, just for something to do.

Amy took a seat at the table. 'I came to apologise,' she said.

Hope kept her back turned and said nothing. She was not going to accept the apology and pretend that made everything all right.

'I know an apology isn't enough,' said Amy, her voice low. 'I suppose I should explain, too.'

Hope swung round. 'An explanation won't be enough, either. You left me with nothing! You stole from me! You destroyed *Material Things*!'

'I didn't think you would have to close the shop,' said Amy, her voice still low. 'I suppose I should have realised, but I convinced myself you'd be able to carry on. That you'd be better off without me.'

Hope made two mugs of coffee and banged them down on the table.

'I couldn't possibly carry on. We were bankrupt.' Her voice was quieter now. What was the point of shouting at Amy? It changed nothing.

'I knew the shop was doing well,' said Amy in that same low voice. 'Yes it was doing well, Hope, thanks to you. You didn't need me there at all.'

'It was a partnership,' said Hope. She wasn't going to accept this from Amy, a pretence that her leaving was for the best. 'Anyway, if you wanted out why didn't you just say so? Then maybe we could have salvaged something. As it was . . . ' Hope shuddered. She really didn't want to remember the shock of finding herself alone.

'I needed the money,' said Amy, her voice so quiet now Hope could hardly hear her. 'At least, Steve did. He convinced me that as half the business was mine I could take the cash and leave you with the rest.' Hope gave an exclamation of disbelief and Amy hurried on. 'I know, I know, I see now I made it impossible for you, but I wanted to believe him so I pretended he was right.'

Hope stirred her coffee and said nothing.

'He wanted the money to invest in his brother's mini-cab business,' said Amy. 'And the business is doing quite well,' she said. 'We're having to work hard but Steve and his brother think they can make a go of it.'

This time Hope did look up. Amy was now part of a successful venture whilst she, Hope, had dealt with the collapse of their last one and had lost the majority of her own money in doing so. 'That must be nice for you,' she said bitterly.

Amy's expression had brightened as she spoke of her boyfriend, but now she looked down again. 'They asked me to join them as a third partner. That's when I realised I had to sort things out with you and *Material Things*. It was quite a shock when I went back to Brighton and found it gone. Then I made enquiries and discovered what had happened. Honestly, Hope, I never thought you'd have to close it down.'

'Without the money you had taken it was bankrupt,' said Hope. 'If you can't afford to pay your suppliers you can't carry on, can you?'

'I didn't think,' said Amy. None of her normal exuberance was showing. Maybe she was truly sorry, but Hope couldn't help feeling angrier than ever. Amy, in the long run, had come out of this very well.

Amy continued, 'Your accountant, Mr Grainger, he explained it all to me. He really doesn't like me, does he?' She gave a brief smile at that. 'Whereas he can't praise you enough. He explained that if it hadn't been for your actions both you and I could have been prevented from being involved in future businesses, because of this one going in to liquidation. He explained that you'd effectively used your own money and that by doing so you'd saved my name as well as your own. And he said you could take out a private prosecution against me, and he was encouraging you to do so.'

Hope said nothing. She was annoyed at Tommy Grainger for explaining so much, although she supposed he had no choice. Amy had legally been a partner in the business.

Now Amy looked straight at Hope. 'Are you going to sue me for the money?'

'No, of course not.' Hope shook her long hair back from her face. 'Mr. Grainger knows that already. All I want to do is put the whole affair behind me.'

Amy smiled properly for the first time. 'I knew it. I knew I could rely on you.'

'I didn't do it for your sake,' said Hope, just wishing the girl would go. She had got what she wanted, hadn't she? A promise of no prosecution, the chance to go ahead and involve herself in another business. 'And I hope you know what you're getting into with Steve and his brother. Can they trust you after this? And do you trust them?'

'Yes, I told you, Steve's turned over a new leaf. His brother was always the sensible one and he's really pleased that Steve is settling down.' She put out her left hand for Hope to see. 'And we're getting married. Of course I trust him.'

Hope shrugged. It was really nothing to do with her. 'Congratulations,' she said dully. 'I wish you well.' It looked like everything was turning out fine for Amy, whilst she, Hope, was still struggling to know what to do with her life.

'Thanks,' said Amy, smiling down at the ring. She took a few sips of her coffee, which must by now be cold. She seemed to have relaxed, as though now everything was explained they could both be happy.

Hope checked her watch, wishing the

Jacksons would hurry up and come back.

'The mini-cab business is doing all right, but we don't have a lot of spare cash,' said Amy.

Hope said nothing. What did that have to do with her?

'But I want to try and make amends.' Amy picked up her handbag and took out an envelope. She pushed it across the table to Hope. 'There's a cheque for five hundred pounds. I know it's nothing to what I owe you, but it's a start. I'm going to try and pay you that every so often until I get to the amount Mr Grainger says you could have claimed off me.'

Hope was speechless. She didn't pick up the envelope, merely stared at it. She had never expected to get the money back. But this wasn't just about money, it was about Amy trying to put things right. Hope could feel a lump in her throat. 'Thanks,' she managed. 'I, er, thanks.'

Amy leant back in her chair and

began to peer around the kitchen. 'So, tell me how you are. Quite a nice set up you've got here. Your Aunt Susie says you're working for some old man? And he's got a grandson about your age? What's he like? Any possibilities there?'

Hope shook her head. She had forgotten this side of Amy, her rampant curiosity and desire to partner Hope off with any single man. 'Here they are now, you can see for yourself,' she said. She was quite happy to introduce Mark Jackson to Amy. Robbie would have been another matter entirely. She didn't know quite what her feelings were for Robbie Mackenzie, but they were too fragile for Amy's kind of teasing.

* * *

Hope was finally going to call on Mrs Slater. She had been putting it off for a while, but with young Mark Jackson constantly trying to persuade her to go out with him she decided that it might be a good idea to get away from

Kirkside for a while.

She got Mrs Slater's phone number from Susie and phoned ahead to make sure this morning was suitable for visiting. The daughter assured her it was and that her mother would be delighted to see Hope.

'She talked about you a lot, after seeing you at the wedding.'

Hope wasn't sure if this was a good thing or not. Mrs Slater was intimidating. But she was committed now and had to go.

Mrs Slater's daughter ushered Hope into a small, over-heated sitting room at the back of the bungalow. The old lady was seated in a high-backed armchair with a rug across her knees, although Hope didn't see how she could possibly be cold.

'Here's Hope McIlroy to see you,' said the daughter heartily. She was in her seventies, but she seemed sprightly.

'I thought you were never going to visit,' said Mrs Slater, eyeing Hope in that disconcerting way.

'I, er, it's good of you to see me.'

'Sit you down, sit you down. I can't be doing with people who hover.'

'I'll make a nice pot of tea, shall I?' said the daughter, and withdrew without waiting for an answer.

'So you want me to tell you about your family, do you?' said Mrs Slater, coming straight to the point.

'Well, yes. I've realised how little I know about them. And Mr Jackson said you might remember.'

'Might! Of course I remember! My brain's as good now as it was fifty years ago, which is more than can be said for some people.'

Hope smiled weakly and wondered if she had made a mistake in coming. Mrs Slater might remember all sorts of things, but did Hope really want to know?

'So you never knew your mother wasn't adopted?' Mrs Slater rubbed her hands together in glee. 'All those years and she never told you?'

'That's right. I didn't know anything

until Susie Ashbury spoke about it, a few months ago.'

'Your mother was a fool not to tell you herself. And to let it cause a rift with your grandmother.'

'My mother must have been very upset about the whole thing,' said Hope, suddenly wanting to defend her mother.

'Too soft she was. Life's tough and you've got to be able to take the knocks. And it wasn't such a very bad thing, was it? She was brought up in a nice house with parents who took good care of her. What did she have to complain about?'

'But the dishonesty . . . ' protested Hope.

'Aye, well, not everyone's as honest as they should be, that's true. And it was different in those days. Appearance was very important.' The old woman cackled, getting into her stride now. 'I could tell you things that would make your hair curl, but none of it was spoken of in public.'

She was interrupted by the arrival of the tea tray. The daughter must have overheard the last sentence because she said, 'I think Hope wanted to know about her own family, Mother, not about the rest of the village. Now how do you take your tea, Hope? Milk? Sugar?'

Mrs Slater fortunately seemed to take the hint. When their conversation resumed she returned to their original topic.

'As I said, your mother was a nice lassie, but soft. Now Jane Calvert, Irving that was, she was another kettle of fish. She lost her mother when she was wee. Jane had a hard time of it, with that old besom for a father. She was a pretty one was Jane, and he'd hardly let her out of his sight. No wonder she didn't get engaged for all those years. She and Joe Calvert were sweet on each other, but her dad thought he wasn't good enough. A few too many airs and graces he had, for just a tailor, although he did sew for the gentry, so I'm told.'

Hope tucked away this little piece of information. Jane's father, Matthew, hadn't just been a village tailor, he had worked for the gentry. She found little tidbits such as this fascinating.

'As I said, Jane had a hard time of it after her mother died. Matthew Irving wasn't the sociable kind. Didn't even let her spend time with his own sister, who would have helped out if he'd allowed it. You know Matthew's sister married a Jackson, don't you? But Matthew didn't approve, goodness knows why not, I've been trying to remember, but if I ever knew it's gone now. I believe they hardly spoke in later life . . . '

Hope hardly heard the last sentences. She was trying to make sense of an earlier one. 'You said Jane's aunt married a Jackson? You don't mean a relative of my Mr Jackson?'

Mrs Slater nodded, eyes sparkling. 'Aye, I believe so. Give me a minute and I'll work out the connection. Don't tell me you didn't know?'

Hope couldn't think of a thing to say. Her head was spinning. Could she really be related to Mr Jackson, and neither of them had known?

Mrs Slater was silent for a moment, counting on her fingers.

'I think this is how it was. Matthew had a much older sister who married a Jackson, William or Billy I think he was. Your Mr Jackson will be their grandson . . . no, it must be great-grandson. Yes, that'll be right.'

'So my great-great-something aunt was his great-grandmother? Are you sure?'

'I may be getting on, but I'm not losing my marbles, young lady! Far from it. Sometimes I think I'm the only one in this village who remembers these things.'

'But why didn't Mr Jackson say anything to me?'

'Because he didn't know, or didn't remember, like I said.' Mrs Slater was back to looking rather smug. 'Not everyone takes the interest I do. I knew as soon as I saw you and you reminded me of Jane I could tell you things. It's taken me a while to remember it all, but there you are.'

Hope wished she had brought her notebook with her. It was all too complicated and too surprising to take in. But one thing seemed pretty clear. She and the Jacksons were related. Distantly, but related nevertheless!

She felt excited, but also confused. Suddenly, from having no family at all, she seemed to have masses. All with stories to their names, whole histories she had known nothing about. And what on earth would Mr Jackson think? What if he didn't want to be related to her?

She took her leave soon after, saying she didn't want to tire Mrs Slater, although if the truth was told the old lady seemed as bright as ever, delighted with the impact of her tales. It was Hope who needed a break. Unfortunately, as she walked down the road past the Ashburys' bungalow Susie appeared at the door.

Susie had been waiting for Hope so she could have a word with her.

'She might not want to talk to you,' Simon had warned.

'Why on earth not?'

'You don't know what Mrs Slater will have said to her.'

But Susie couldn't imagine old Mrs Slater would say anything worrying. Hope had got over her initial shock of finding she had had a 'proper' family in St. Ann's Bridge. Now she was doing exactly what she should be doing, making enquiries, finding out about her roots. And her roots were here. Susie just hoped her goddaughter would realise this and decide to stay.

She hurried down the steps as Hope approached. 'I saw you go up to Mrs Slater. How did you get on? Do come in and tell me.'

'I should probably be getting back . . .'

Susie was prepared for this prevarication. It was lucky she had been sitting at the front window and had therefore seen Andrew Jackson's hired car go past. 'I saw Mr Jackson go along the road with his son not ten minutes ago, so you've no need to rush. In you come, Simon's in the conservatory, come on through.'

Hope followed her godmother reluctantly into the house.

'Why don't you stay for lunch?' said Susie happily. 'Just soup and a sandwich? Yes? I'll put the soup on and be with you in a second. You go and say hello to Simon.'

When she joined the two they were talking about the new golf course that had opened near Dumfries and which Simon was eager to try. Susie couldn't understand why her husband would think Hope was interested in that and immediately changed the subject.

'How did you get on with Mrs Slater?'

'Fine. She's very impressive for her age, isn't she? I believe she's in her nineties but there's certainly nothing wrong with her memory.'

'I'm so pleased she agreed to talk to you. She can sometimes be a little awkward.'

Hope pulled a face at this and Susie began to feel worried. Surely old Mrs Slater couldn't really have remembered anything that would upset Hope?

'Did she remember your grandparents?'

'Yes.' Hope pushed the long hair back from her face and frowned, as though going over it all in her head. 'And my great-grandfather.'

'Sometimes family things are best left alone,' said Simon. Susie glared at him.

Hope said, 'My grandfather seems to have been rather nice, actually. Mrs Slater certainly liked him. And she made me feel sorry for my grandmother, Jane. I had been a little bitter about her, but it seems she had a hard time from her dad, my great-grandfather.'

Susie nodded approvingly. 'There are always reasons for things.'

'What really surprised me,' said Hope

slowly, 'Was that apparently my great-grandfather was related to the Jacksons. Did you know that?'

Now it was Susie's turn to be surprised. My goodness! But on the other hand, of course. Weren't many of the old village families related? She should have thought of it herself.

'No, I didn't know, but I suppose it's not so very unlikely. What was the relationship, did she say? How far back does it go?'

'Quite a way.' Hope shook her head, bemused. 'I'll have to work it out properly.'

'Maybe this explains why you and Mr Jackson hit it off right from the start.' Hope looked doubtful but Susie hurried on. 'Now you'll have even more in common. I wonder if he knows? Probably not, or I'm sure he'd have said. He'll be so pleased.'

'Mmm,' said Hope.

'All the more reason for you to stay in the area,' continued Susie happily. She couldn't believe how well the visit to Mrs Slater had gone. 'Gosh, Robbie will be happy.'

Hope frowned. Maybe Susie was going too fast for her. 'You and Robbie are getting on well, aren't you?' said Susie encouragingly. 'How's he enjoying his course?'

'How should I know, Susie? We're just friends, nothing more. I haven't heard a word from him since he went away.'

Susie was flummoxed. That didn't sound like Robbie. She could have sworn the romance between the two young people had been progressing, slowly it was true, but still progressing. And Maria certainly thought so.

Robbie Returns From Wales

To Hope's relief, Mr Jackson was delighted with the news they were related. Once he'd mulled over what Mrs Slater has told her, he admitted he vaguely remembered something about a rift in the family, but said he'd had no idea it had any connection with Matthew Irving.

He patted her hand. 'The Jacksons have never had many children, only one a generation for as long as I can mind, until Andrew's brood came along. I've never had a cousin before, or nephews and nieces. And now I've got you.'

He was so serious Hope felt tears rise to her eyes. He wasn't given to great shows of emotion, but allowed her to squeeze his hand in return and she whispered, 'Thank you.'

She wondered what his son and grandson would make of it all. She would hate them to think she was trying to elbow her way into the family, claiming to be a long lost relative. Mark, however, seemed to find the news highly amusing, and Andrew was quietly welcoming.

'We know you'll keep an eye on Dad whether this had come up or not, but it's nice to feel there's a special connection,' he said, kissing her on the cheek.

Unfortunately not everyone in the village was so positive. When she went to the post office a couple of days later the conversation ceased as she opened the door. After a moment it restarted and Mrs Robson behind the counter offered Hope congratulations on her new-found relatives. 'It's surprising you didn't know before, isn't it?' she added, keeping her eyes on Hope's face. 'Are you sure your mother hadn't mentioned . . . ?'

'Such a lucky coincidence, you

ending up in the house there. Why, you won't need to look for anywhere else to live now, will you?' said one of the other ladies. 'I wonder what young Andrew Jackson thinks . . . '

Hope hated the implications. They were totally wrong. She didn't expect or want anything from the Jacksons, but people were naturally suspicious. Susie didn't help by telling anyone who wanted to listen how pleased she was to have brought Hope to Kirkside where she clearly belonged.

'It's not for ever,' said Hope irritably.

★ ★ ★

Robbie was finally back from Wales. He set off immediately for Kirkside. The course had been excellent and had kept him very busy, but the thought of Hope had been constantly in his mind. He had tried to phone her a number of times, but either there was no answer or he ended up speaking to an Australian boy. After twice leaving her a message to phone him back, he had given up. She must be busy with Mr Jackson's son and grandson. At least he hoped that was the reason.

It wasn't Hope who opened the impressive front door, as he had come to expect. It was a young man of about Robbie's own age, with rather long bleached-blond hair.

'G'day,' he said, smiling broadly and showing very white teeth. 'Can I help you?' His attitude was casual and friendly and Robbie immediately disliked him.

'I came by to see Hope,' he said. 'Is she in?'

'Of course. Come through, we're all in the kitchen.' The man spoke with a marked Australian accent which in anyone else Robbie would have found quite pleasant. He wore a faded short-sleeved T shirt and torn jeans. His feet were bare, which was really a bit of an affectation on a cold day like this one. 'When I say all, I mean me and Hope and my dad. Not the old man, he's having one of his lie-downs, but I don't suppose you wanted to see him, did you?'

'I'm always happy to have a chat with Mr Jackson,' said Robbie stiffly.

They entered the kitchen to find Hope sitting at the table leafing through a recipe book beside an older man, presumably Mr Jackson's son, reading a newspaper.

Hope looked up, but before she could say anything the irritating young man had jumped in again. 'We've just had a cuppa, but I could put the kettle on again if you'd like?'

'Er, nothing, thanks. I won't stay long. Hello, Hope. How are you doing?'

'Fine, fine. Have you met Mr Jackson's son and grandson? This is Andrew, and this is Mark.'

After greeting the two men he turned again to Hope, but before he could speak Mark jumped in again. 'Have you heard our news?'

He put a hand on Hope's shoulder and Robbie felt the world spin for a moment, dreading what might come next. What possible news could they be about to announce? Surely nothing could have happened this quickly?

'We're family,' explained Andrew with a smile.

'We're related, aren't we, cuz?' said Mark, giving Hope a hug. 'Hope found that our great-great-something or other was her great aunt. Or something. Pretty cool, huh?'

Robbie could hardly speak for the relief. He would prefer it if Hope wasn't related to this bumptious young man, but it could have been so much worse. He made himself say, 'Well that's very interesting. And such a coincidence, Hope, you coming to live at Kirkside.'

Hope looked at him suspiciously, as though he was implying something. 'Coincidences do happen, you know.'

'Yes, of course, I didn't mean . . . '

But it wasn't long before the younger man had bounced back in to the conversation. 'It's been quite a holiday, all in all. Interesting seeing the old place, and finding long lost cousins is even better.' He swung one of the kitchen chairs around and sat on it back-to-front. 'But boy how can you cope with the weather? And it isn't even winter yet, so they say. I've been telling Hope she should come out to Oz and see what sunshine is really like.' He gave a brilliant smile across the table to Hope. She returned it, less enthusiastically, but she did give him a smile. Robbie would have preferred to have her attention on him.

'It's true, Australia isn't a bad place,' said Andrew. 'Hope would be very welcome to visit.'

'I'm not planning to travel at the moment,' said Hope in her quiet voice. 'Mr Jackson may be getting a lot better, but he's not well enough to be left on his own yet.'

'You should come over as soon as you're free,' said Mark. 'You can stay with us as long as you like.'

This talk of Hope visiting Australia filled Robbie once again with horror. It was just over a fortnight since he had last seen her. Surely things couldn't have changed so quickly? Mark Jackson seemed hardly to be able to take his eyes off her, but she couldn't see anything in this jumped up puppy. Could she?

He cleared his throat. 'There's a new film on in Dumfries on Saturday,' he said, addressing Hope. 'I've heard it's good, an improvement on that weird one we saw last time. I wondered if you'd like to go?'

Once again Mark jumped in before anyone else could speak. 'Saturday's no good mate. It's our last evening here and we're all going out for a slap-up family meal, even the old guy has agreed to come. Give Hope a break from cooking for us all.'

Hope said nothing.

'Oh, well, never mind,' said Robbie, suddenly angry. If Hope couldn't be bothered to answer him herself she couldn't be that interested, could she? He was hurt, but he didn't want her to see that. He made his excuses and left soon after. Obviously, now she had found her long lost family, she had no time left for him.

★ ★ ★

Hope was in a quandary about so many things. She was touched and relieved that Amy was back in touch and that she intended to repay some of the money. And it was interesting to find out more about her family, but each new discovery seemed to knock her sideways, to force her to re-evaluate once again who she was.

She didn't know why the fact she was related to the Jacksons seemed to be such a big thing, but it was. It tied her more closely than ever to Scotland and to St. Ann's Bridge.

Which brought her to the question of Cleughbrae. It was confusing, having the possibility of buying it thrust upon her. She hadn't been considering buying anything, least of all here. The question hadn't even arisen, as she knew she couldn't afford it. Now, with the remainder of her savings plus the money promised by Amy, it was a possibility, as long as she also found some work. But was that what she wanted? She really didn't know.

The obvious interest from Mark Jackson was more a minor irritation than another quandary. He wasn't her type. Seeing him and Robbie Mackenzie together merely confirmed that. For all her current confusion, Robbie was the one who seemed real. Mark was nothing more than a boy. She didn't take his constant invitations seriously, but she was pleased when he and his father left for the airport. It was one less thing to have to cope with.

Mr Jackson had enjoyed their visit but he still tired easily. On the day following his son's departure, he went as usual to lie down for his afternoon rest. Hope decided to take Lucy out for a walk, to try to clear her thoughts.

It was only mid-afternoon but by this

time in the year the light was beginning to fade. There was a hint of frost in the air and Hope pulled the soft velvet hat low over her ears. She had on a long black woollen coat — boring but sensible — and had brightened it up with the purple hat and a multi-coloured scarf her mother had knitted at her request many years ago.

Lucy walked slowly at her heel, looking at the ground a yard or so ahead of her. It seemed impossible that the dog could actually see anything through that shaggy grey fur, but she never stumbled.

As Hope turned down the heavily overhung track to Cleughbrae, she realised this was the first time she had come here on her own. The first visit had been with Susie and she had felt uneasy. On the second, with Robbie, her curiosity had been aroused, but she had still been cautious.

Today, she just wanted to see the place again and work out how she really felt about it. She didn't have a key. She didn't need to go inside to do this. She would know just by seeing it.

And she did.

In the hazy mist and near-darkness, with the yellow and red and bronze of the trees all around, the tiny house stood proudly in its place. It was a little dilapidated, a little in need of some love, but with its soft pink stonework and fancy eaves, it was beautiful.

'I could live here,' said Hope to Lucy, who looked up questioningly. 'Yes, I could definitely live here.'

Somehow the place was right. Hope didn't feel nervous in the gloom. The isolation only made it more perfect, although it had taken the weeks of living in Mr Jackson's relatively lonely house for her to realise this was what she liked. She walked around the building twice and then sat down on the rickety bench where she and Susie had rested so many months before.

'But I'll need to work out the finances first,' she confided to Lucy. 'I don't think I can rely on Amy continuing to pay me regularly, although it would be nice if she did. I need to find a way of earning money, here in St. Ann's Bridge. Or at least nearby.'

Lucy pushed her nose against Hope's gloved hand, as though agreeing. Hope felt suddenly light-hearted. She had made a decision, and it had nothing to do with Robbie Mackenzie. If he couldn't be bothered to phone her, that was his problem, not hers.

'I've got one or two ideas,' continued Hope. 'How about you?'

Lucy sighed and lay down at her feet. Apparently she thought Hope capable of sorting this out all on her own.

* * *

For the first time, Robbie was beginning to regret taking on this new job. It seemed to involve far too many late nights, which made it impossible to catch up with Hope. He knew he needed to speak to her in person, to find out if she really was avoiding him.

And then when he wasn't working, there was the band event he had agreed to do with *Abhainn*.

As they were performing original material they needed to practice together. This took up even more of his free time. He wanted to scream, but he had promised to help and couldn't back out now.

The very last thing he expected, when he returned home after final practice one Saturday, was for his mother to tell him Hope had called by.

'Hope came here? Was she looking for me?' Suddenly the world felt a brighter place.

'I'm not sure,' said his mother, smiling at his enthusiasm. 'Maybe she was just walking Lucy. But she came in for a cup of coffee.'

'How is she?' It felt far longer than a week since Robbie had seen her. 'At least those Australians will have gone back by now.'

'That's right. That must mean less work for Hope, although she's not one to complain.'

'Did she say anything about them?'

'Not really.' His mother looked amused. 'Should she have?'

'You know they're related, don't you? That grandson of Mr Jackson's was pretty keen on her, wouldn't leave her alone from what I could see.' It was a relief for Robbie to be able to put this into words. The worry over Mark Jackson had been festering within him. 'I bet she's glad to see the back of him.' And now she had come looking for him! He pushed aside his empty plate and reached for the biscuit tin. He hadn't realised how hungry he was.

'She didn't mention him at all. And if he was a little keen, which isn't surprising with a pretty girl like Hope, I've no doubts Hope can take care of herself. She's quiet, but she's not soft.'

'No, that's true,' said Robbie, relieved. 'Did she ask after me?'

'She didn't need to. I told her you were away practicing for the band night tonight.'

'Oh.' This just served to remind

Robbie that he only had an hour to change and get back out to join the band. Should he have invited Hope along? And yet if he had, and by some miracle she had said yes, he would be on stage for quite a lot of the time so would hardly see her.

*　　*　　*

Hope was at a loose end. Somehow, she had thought Robbie might come round and visit her once the Australians had left. Hadn't he said he would? Now she had got over the shock of finding more relatives, live ones this time, she wanted to talk it over with him. Even if he hadn't phoned whilst he was away, he was still her best friend in St. Ann's Bridge. For a while she had decided not to seek him out, just because Susie was so keen on pushing them together. Today she had decided that was ridiculous and she should do what she wanted. So she had 'happened' to take Lucy a walk in the direction of Holm

Farm, but he hadn't been home.

'What's wrong with you?' snapped Mr Jackson when she got up for the fifth time to straighten the curtains. 'Can't keep still today. Don't tell me you're missing that grandson of mine?'

Hope assured him that although it had been lovely to meet Andrew and Mark, she certainly wasn't missing them.

'Maybe you need to take yourself out for the evening. Can't be any fun for you, stuck in here with an old man like me. What's happened to that Robbie Mackenzie? I thought he was showing an interest?'

This really wasn't the sort of conversation Hope wanted to have and she was relieved when the phone rang. She had to go out into the hall to answer it, Kirkside not being the sort of house to have portable handsets.

'Hello, is that Hope? It's Claire Mackenzie here. Do you remember me?'

Hope certainly remembered Robbie's

new sister-in-law, but she couldn't think of any reason why the girl should be phoning her. 'Yes, of course. I had a lovely time at your wedding.'

'Thank you. So did I! In a way, that's why I'm phoning. Do you remember the band that played in the evening, the one where Robbie had to help out by playing fiddle?'

'Yes, they were good. Some kind of gaelic name.'

'That's right, *Abhainn*. They're competing in a 'Battle of the Bands' evening in Dumfries tonight, and have asked Robbie to join them to strengthen their line up. Luke and I thought we'd go along to listen and we wondered if you would like to come too? That is, if you don't have anything else on. I know it's very last minute, but we've only just decided to go ourselves.'

'That's very kind of you,' said Hope, hunting around for a good reason to decline. She was fed up with being pushed. And then she thought, why shouldn't she go? She wanted to see

Robbie again, and that was what mattered. 'Yes, I'd love to. What time were you thinking of going?'

★ ★ ★

The 'battle' was taking place in an elegant red-sandstone hall on the edge of the town. It was an impressive venue, with plenty of car-parking space, already well-filled. Once inside Hope had little time to appreciate the rather grand décor as Luke went to buy them drinks and Claire encouraged her to push as near to the front as possible. The place was busy with crowds of teenagers interspersed with more elderly people such as themselves.

'What actually is a Battle of the Bands?' asked Hope.

'To tell you the truth, I'm not quite sure.' Claire broke off to greet a number of acquaintances and took the opportunity to question them. 'Apparently it's a competition for any local band who want to try and get some publicity. In somewhere like Glasgow it might end up with the band being signed to a record label, but down here I think it's more for the kudos.'

Luke joined them and handed the girls their drinks, then pulled a typed sheet of paper from his pocket. 'Looks like they've got quite a number of entries. At least twelve, the barman said. *Abhainn* are on third and if they get through the first round they'll be on again after the break.'

Hope glanced nervously at her watch. Mr Jackson had insisted she stay out as long as she wanted, but she hadn't anticipated being very late. She did, of course, have her mobile with her, but she knew how reluctant he was to contact her on that.

But she forgot all this once the music started. She had assumed the music would be Scottish traditional, but this didn't seem to be the case at all. The first group were a bunch of teenagers who tried their best to play very loudly. They were enthusiastic and noisy, if not exactly skilled.

Hope couldn't help grinning and felt herself getting into the swing of things. She didn't have to be here just to see Robbie, she could enjoy herself as well.

The second band were even noisier and she wasn't sorry when their three-song set came to an end. Luke pointed out the judges who were sitting to one side of the stage. One had his hands over his ears, so Hope presumed this group wouldn't be going through to the next round.

And then it was the turn of *Abhainn*. They looked far older than the others, and very different in their kilts. There were a number of catcalls from the audience, who obviously hadn't been expecting this kind of music. But once Sam introduced the first number, a silence fell.

This music was totally unlike what they had played at Luke and Claire's wedding. The feel might be Scottish-traditional, but it also had a new edge to it. Sam sang in his pronounced

Scottish accent, a contrast to the pseudo-American of the earlier bands, and he was in tune, too. But it was the energy of the fiddle playing, the beat of the drum, that carried the song along. At the end the audience applauded rapturously. Hope almost shouted herself hoarse, clapping until her hands were sore.

'Pretty good, hey?' said Luke, when they could speak again. 'He's not bad with the fiddle, my wee brother.'

'They were all brilliant,' said Claire happily. 'They're bound to get through to the next stage. That'll show those youngsters that crashing around with a guitar isn't the only way to be a star.'

Privately, Hope thought Robbie looked a hundred times more handsome than the youths with their long hair and shiny shirts. *Abhainn* had teamed up their kilts with heavy boots and black T shirts. They looked both stylish and slightly dangerous.

And then she had no more chance to dwell on that, because she realised

Robbie had spotted them and was pushing his way towards them through the crowd.

* * *

Robbie couldn't believe it when he saw Luke and Claire and Hope standing in the crowd. They were slightly to one side, but Luke had waved wildly to him, so it wasn't hard to spot them. What on earth were they doing here?

'I didn't expect to see you,' he said, slapping his brother on the back. He suddenly found he wasn't sure how to greet Hope, so merely smiled at her.

'You didn't even tell us you were playing,' said Claire accusingly. 'If your mum hadn't said, we wouldn't have known. But I'm so glad we came, you were excellent.'

'Which is more than you can say for some of the other bands,' said Luke.

Robbie didn't want to be disloyal to his fellow performers, but secretly he felt Luke was right. A girl of around twenty had now taken the stage. She had pink and blue hair and an unusual, triangular-shaped guitar.

'I think I'll go and get myself a drink,' Robbie said, looking for an excuse to extract himself from the crush. 'I'm not needed back on stage until the break.'

He was wondering how he could get Hope to go with him, without making a big issue of it, when she said, 'I'll come with you. I could do with a bit more space.'

Claire and Luke exchanged looks which made Robbie wonder exactly what his mother had said to them. They claimed they were happy to stay where they were and 'enjoy' the music. Robbie took Hope's hand and began to make his way through the crowd.

He ordered the drinks and then they went to stand against the wall at the back of the room. The music was still loud, but it was no longer ear-shattering.

'I hope we sounded better than this,' he said, frowning at another missed note. 'They didn't give us much time to do sound checks.'

'You were brilliant,' said Hope. 'Easily the best so far.'

Robbie's spirits rose immeasurably. The band felt their set had gone pretty well, but praise from Hope was more important.

They stood in silence for a while, but it felt to Robbie to be an easy silence. Whatever awkwardness there had been between them had fallen away.

'It's good to see you again,' he said, during the next break in the music.

Hope raised her eyebrows. She had tied her hair back in a loose plait and for once you could see all of her face quite clearly. 'I haven't been anywhere,' she said.

'But you've been busy, with Mr Jackson, and your relatives.' He took a deep breath. 'At least, I presume that was why you didn't want to speak to me?'

'Who said I didn't want to speak to you?' Hope looked puzzled. She had such an open face and he could read all her emotions on it. 'I suppose you were busy while you were away, but you did say you were going to phone. Although there was no reason why you should . . .'

'But I did,' said Robbie. 'I left messages for you. Twice. Didn't you get them?'

Hope shook her head slowly. 'I didn't get any messages. Who did you leave them with?'

'I presume it was Mr Jackson's grandson, from the accent.'

'Ah.'

'I think he quite liked you.' Robbie couldn't help his tone sounding accusing.

'He was a nice enough boy. But far too young for me.'

Finally Robbie could feel himself relaxing. He was furious the boy hadn't passed on his messages, but that was over now. Hope hadn't been avoiding him. He bent and caressed her hair with his cheek. 'I'm so glad.'

Hope smiled again. She seemed to like to be near him. And then she sighed. 'A lot has happened recently. Amy turned up at Kirkside — you remember I told you about my so-called business partner? And then there's Cleughbrae. And then all the family things.'

Robbie sighed too. He'd somehow hoped that they could forget all the complications of Hope's life and simply get on with being the two of them. He should have known it wouldn't be so easy.

'What on earth did Amy want?' He listened whilst she explained, pleased that some things were going better for her. They talked about this for a while, and then he asked, 'How do you feel about having a family connection to the Jacksons? You'd found out from Mrs Slater. Is that right?'

Hope nodded. 'Yes. It's quite amazing, really, isn't it?' She shook her head. 'I'm pleased, of course I am, but I know some people think I knew already and I

292

came up here to wheedle my way into his life. You said yourself it was rather too much of a coincidence, me ending up here, didn't you?'

'I didn't mean that,' he said, horrified.

'You might not, but others do. Fortunately not Mr Jackson or Andrew or even Mark. And the other thing is, I keep thinking, why didn't I know this? What else don't I know? My dad's family were so simple compared to all this.'

'Does it matter?'

'It confuses me.'

'Just relax. You'll get used to it.' Robbie felt angry that she could suspect him of suspecting her, but he could also feel some sympathy. She was such an honest person, she would hate people to think those things. He put one arm around her, wishing there was somewhere to put down his glass. 'It's not all bad. You're related to a really nice family. You definitely belong in the village now.'

She sighed then, and leant her head on his shoulder. He wished he knew if this meant she was relaxing as he advised, or whether she would like to but couldn't.

'Hope, we need to go somewhere we can talk properly.'

But before she could answer Sam appeared behind them. 'Robbie! Goodness, man, I've been looking for you everywhere. They're going to start the judging soon and we need to be back up there. Can't you leave this lovey-dovey stuff for some other time?'

Hope moved away from him. 'Sorry. I should have known you were busy.'

'Yes, but we still need to talk.'

'Robbie, come on!'

'I'll see you later,' said Robbie to Hope, desperate not to let her go without something being agreed.

'I don't know how long we're staying. I should really get back for Mr Jackson.'

'Tomorrow, then,' said Robbie. I'll come and see you in the morning. Are you around?'

'Yes, I'll be there.' She smiled, a proper, warm smile. 'I'll look forward to it. And I'm so glad I came tonight.'

'So am I . . . ' There was so much more Robbie wanted to say, but he was being towed away toward the stage door by an increasingly irate Sam.

The rest of the evening passed in a daze. *Abhainn* did very well in the 'battle', coming second overall, and Robbie was pleased for them. But most of all he was pleased that he was close to resolving something with Hope.

But nervous, too. What exactly were they going to resolve?

⋆ ⋆ ⋆

Mr Jackson seemed to sense something was worrying Hope, although she didn't actually mention to him she was expecting Robbie to visit. When Robbie appeared, at about ten o'clock, he gave a sigh of relief. 'So that's what you've been waiting for,' he said. He picked up the one walking stick which was all he now needed to get around. 'Well, I'll leave you two young people in peace. Pass me the newspaper, will you? I'll take that through to the sitting room.'

'Actually, I was wondering about going out for a walk,' said Robbie, not taking his eyes off Hope.

She smiled. 'I was thinking exactly the same thing. It's such a lovely sunny day we should make the most of it.'

'Don't take Lucy if you're going far,' said Mr Jackson, putting a hand on the old dog's head. 'She's not up to long walks.'

'I don't think we'll go far,' said Robbie.

Once they were outside, Hope in her woollen coat and bright scarf, he said, 'I thought we could go to Cleughbrae?'

Hope nodded. Somehow, she had known this was what he would suggest.

They walked hand in hand in silence for a while.

As they turned down the now familiar track, Hope said, 'Mr Jackson was just pointing out an advert to me in the local paper. Apparently one of the colleges is introducing a textile-related course. They aren't actually advertising for staff, but he thinks I should get in touch and see if there is an opening for me.'

'Excellent idea,' said Robbie, smiling down at her. 'Anything that keeps you in the area is good, as far as I'm concerned.'

'I've decided to stay here if I can,' said Hope, not looking at him. She didn't want him to think he was the reason. 'I think I reached the decision a while ago, although I didn't want to admit it. I don't want to be too far away from Mr Jackson, or from Susie, for all her annoying interfering ways.' Hope thought of how Susie pushing her so hard in Robbie's direction had almost made her do the opposite. Thank goodness she had gone to that band night!

'And me?' said Robbie. They had reached the clearing and he stopped and took hold of both her hands.

They were standing so close that it almost took Hope's breath away. She wanted to lean in to him, to be closer still. But there were things that had to be said first.

'I'd like it if we carried on seeing each other, which we could if I stayed nearby. But I don't want that to be the reason for staying.'

'Why not?' Robbie shook the dark, wavy hair back from his face, frowning down at her.

'It's hard to explain.' Hope disengaged her hands and took a step back, so she could think clearly. 'I've got to make decisions for myself. If I stay here just because of you — and why should I, we're hardly even going out — then I'm relying on you to make things all right. And I don't want that. I want to rely on myself.'

'We all rely on other people,' said Robbie gently. 'There's nothing wrong with that.'

'Maybe it's easier for you. You're used to all this family thing. I've started to think I do have a sense of belonging, here in St. Ann's Bridge, but it scares me too.'

Robbie took a deep breath as though trying to hold on to his patience. Hope knew it was going to be like this. He was annoyed with her.

And then shook his head and said, 'I'm sure you'll get used to this family thing, as you call it. I'm not trying to rush you. I'm prepared to wait.'

Hope thought this over and felt irrationally disappointed. He was very easily persuaded. Maybe he didn't want to be close to her after all?

'That's fine then,' she said brightly. She turned towards the cottage, where Lucy was already snuffling through the fallen leaves. 'Shall we have a look around?'

Robbie took her hand again, seeming not to notice that she was hurt.

She continued brightly, 'I've actually been in touch with the estate and made tentative enquiries about buying it. It would be amazing to live here, if I can be sure I can afford it. Mr Jackson wants to help me buy it, but that's definitely not on. I'd rather take help from Susie than from him, but I'm not letting her interfere either.'

'Sounds good to me. If you can manage on your own, go for it. It's a great wee place.'

He began to talk about the state of the roof and whether some of the trees growing at the back of the house might need to be felled to give more light. It was good he was taking an interest, but surely this wasn't what he had come to talk to her about? It had been no trouble at all to divert him from personal discussion.

Eventually they found themselves sitting on the old garden bench. It was chilly despite the bright sunshine, and Hope didn't object when Robbie put an arm around her.

'I just hope I can afford it,' she said, biting her lip, trying to concentrate on the house and not on the man beside her. 'Mortgages aren't too easy to come by at the moment.'

'You won't need a huge mortgage,' said Robbie easily. 'I'm sure you won't have a problem. Of course, if you took in a lodger, that would help your finances no end.'

'A lodger?' Hope pulled away a little so she could see his face. He was smiling.

'Yes, a lodger. I can think of the perfect one. Me.'

'Robbie!' Hope didn't know what to think. Was this a joke? He pulled her close, resting his cheek on her hair. After seeming to back off without any problem, now she suspected he had just been biding his time. She felt simultaneously excited and scared. He wasn't going to give up so easily.

'It would have to be me. I don't think I could bear a situation like the one at Kirkside, where you had Mark Jackson hassling you to be with him morning noon and night.'

'He didn't hassle me all the time.'

'Even half the time was bad enough.

Don't you think I'd be a good lodger? I'd pay my share of the expenses, and despite what my mother says I'm fairly clean and tidy.'

Hope didn't know what to say. She was sure he would be the perfect lodger, she couldn't think of anyone she would rather share the house with. But would she be able to think of him as just her lodger? Resting in his arms like this she wanted nothing more than to turn and kiss him.

'I don't think your parents would approve,' she said, making an effort to be sensible. 'Even although it would all be above board.'

Robbie dropped a kiss on her lips, just a brief touch, and then moved away so that she could see his face properly. 'Now it's funny you should say that,' he said, but he sounded serious rather than amused. 'Why don't we get married then? That would please a lot of people. My parents. Susie. Mr Jackson. Me. And I had kind of hoped you would like the idea, too. But when you explained about wanting a bit of space, I thought maybe you would prefer it this way first. So the choice is up to you — either way, you'll find it pretty difficult to shift me.'

Yet again, as had happened so often over the last few months, Hope felt the world shift around her and settle into a new reality.

'I love you,' said Robbie, bending to kiss her again. 'Will you please say something?'

'I love you too,' said Hope, because it was the first thing that occurred to her. She smiled slowly. She thought she might like this new reality. 'Maybe you should kiss me once again, and that will help me decide?' She put out her arms to pull him closer. Suddenly she knew what she wanted, exactly what she wanted.

'I know family is important to you,' he said, 'And now we can be one of our own.' He bent his lips to hers.

It was a while before Hope had the chance to speak again. Then she rested her head on his shoulder and said softly, 'A family of my own. You and me will be a real family.'

'I'll take that as a yes, shall I? I don't want you to think I'm rushing you or anything . . .'

'Yes,' said Hope, certain now that she wasn't being rushed. 'Yes, yes, yes.'

THE END

We do hope that you have enjoyed reading this large print book.

Did you know that all of our titles are available for purchase?

We publish a wide range of high quality large print books including:
Romances, Mysteries, Classics
General Fiction
Non Fiction and Westerns

Special interest titles available in large print are:
The Little Oxford Dictionary
Music Book, Song Book
Hymn Book, Service Book

Also available from us courtesy of Oxford University Press:
Young Readers' Dictionary
(large print edition)
Young Readers' Thesaurus
(large print edition)

For further information or a free brochure, please contact us at:
Ulverscroft Large Print Books Ltd.,
The Green, Bradgate Road, Anstey,
Leicester, LE7 7FU, England.
Tel: (00 44) **0116 236 4325**
Fax: (00 44) **0116 234 0205**

Other titles in the
Linford Romance Library:

SPADES AND HEARTS

Wendy Kremer

When Sara takes over her aunt's market garden in a small country village, she becomes a part of village life and loses her heart to James, a customer. James initially doubts her capabilities, but finds he's not just interested in the vegetables from her garden . . . Meanwhile, there is Ken, an old rival of James, and there's also Pamela, James' attractive assistant who wants to be more. Love grows and flourishes. Who will harvest, and who'll be left empty-handed?